THE SUSIE CARSON HISTORY

MYSTERIES

The Fourth of July Can Be Murder!

AUTHOR: DIANNE WARTH-VEREEN

THE SUSIE CARSON HISTORY

MYSTERIES

The Susie Carson History Mystery Series is dedicated to the memory of Susie Sellers Carson of Southport, N.C.   Mrs. Carson lived her life in Southport, N.C., in Brunswick Co., North Carolina's largest county. She became interested in the history of Southport and Brunswick County and eventually became an expert on the subject. She was one of the people responsible for the formation of the Southport Historical Society. She taught Brunswick County history at the local community college and also taught local genealogy there. She was the mother of a daughter, Kathryn Carson Kalmanson, who is a senior research librarian at the University of Maryland, Salisbury. She was a career legal secretary (remembered as working for Bunn Frink and Jimmy Prevatte). The profits from the Susie Carson mysteries go to help fund the Susie Carson Scholarship awarded yearly by the Southport Historical Society to a deserving Brunswick County high school senior.(**Author's Note**). *An author can use a little magic to bring back people and places that are no longer in existence. I have asked and received permission to use names of friends who knew Susie Carson and to also move them from the past to the present, change their ages and sometimes their hair color and height, too. Several people chose to be someone*

AUTHOR: DIANNE WARTH-VEREEN

"else" for a change and so I changed their names per request. You might recognize them anyway but that's ok. Some of my favorite Southport memories were made in places that no longer exist so you might find that the Southport in this series is a mishmash of old and new. Just know I haven't lost my mind; I do know things have changed. Those of us who grew up in Southport in the 40's, 50's and 60's will also recognize places and people who are gone-but- not-forgotten. Like Susie, they populate this world of memory and fiction that is created in an effort to preserve a Southport I grew up in. I miss the people and times and so do many other Southport natives. The thing that we all acknowledge is that the memories we share with one another can never be taken from us and that "our" Southport will always live on. It's my hope that by sharing "our" Southport with those who didn't get a chance to live in it they will understand why we loved it and the people in it so much.

AUTHOR: DIANNE WARTH-VEREEN

Chapter One

C.J. Stone was tired. She had been working so much overtime lately that she often felt she met herself both coming and going. She was a Southport native; born and bred. Only 5'2" tall, with hair that was a beautiful silver color that could never be reproduced from a bottle, C.J. did her utmost to prove herself in a man's world. As the first woman Sheriff of Brunswick County, C.J. felt she often had to work twice as hard and prove herself twice as good as others who'd had her position in the past. It could be tiring. She longed for the time when she had been able to enjoy the 4th of July Festival just like everyone else in town but she had a job to do. She took a sip of iced tea and left enough money on the counter to pay for her lunch. Everything was in order for the biggest weekend of the year in the small sea side town of Southport, N.C. The festival was the oldest continuously running 4th of July celebration in the United States. She never would get used to calling it by its official name, The North Carolina Fourth of July Festival. That was what they named it in 1972. Before that, it was just Southport's 4th of July parade. C.J. and her friend Sparkie Mills were looking at old pictures from the parades

AUTHOR: DIANNE WARTH-VEREEN

of the 50's just the night before. It was hot outside and the Jim Burns said on the noon weather that it would reach 100 for the parade. She noticed strangers and old friends on the sidewalks as she walked toward the office.

"Hi, C.J.", yelled, Joyce, an old friend who was in town for the celebration. It was always fun to see people who had gone to high school with you. You always had to hope that you had aged better than they had. The old school building had almost burned to the ground one winter yet every time she ran into someone from high school they brought it back to life. C.J. still thought the fire was caused by arson although it had never been proven. She wondered if anyone would ever admit to setting the fire. It really didn't matter since the Southport Fire Department under the watchful gaze of Ormond Leggett and Harold Aldridge and all of their volunteer help had managed to save part of it. It wasn't used as the high school any more since the fire but the local classes from the Historical Society were held in the auditorium that still stood as proud as it had for years. The old brick shell stood as a testament to those who had walked its hallowed halls in search of an education.

AUTHOR: DIANNE WARTH-VEREEN

THE SUSIE CARSON HISTORY

MYSTERIES

The scent of chalk and erasers still seemed to permeate the walls, eliciting memories every time it was entered by alumni. Miss Susie Carson was walking up Moore Street from her home. She was dressed in a beautiful navy pants suit with a tri colored blouse in honor of the birthday of America. C.J. wondered if Kathryn, Susie's daughter, had made it for her. Kathryn had a way with a needle that no one except trained designers usually had. Susie was legal secretary to one of the county's premier attorneys. She was often credited with running the entire office. Once she had been forced to go to the Court to ask for continuance for her former employer, Mr. Frink's, cases since he was caught in the embargo against Cuba at the time. The judge had no problem recognizing her in front of the Court. "Come on in, Miss Susie, "the Judge is credited with saying, "We all know who really practices law over there at Mr. Frink's".

Susie was born in Brunswick County and had lived there most of her life except for a short foray during the war years to live in Washington, D.C., with her soldier husband. When it came time to have her daughter, she wanted her to be born in Brunswick County so she returned and had never left again for any

AUTHOR: DIANNE WARTH-VEREEN

long period of time. Everyone knew Miss
Susie. She had taught all of the Baptist
children in Sunday school over the years and
many of the others had been in her G.A.
classes or learned Brunswick County history
at her feet. She had created the first lending
library at the Baptist Church assuring that
the kids had things to read that enhanced
their perception of God and country.

C.J. had heard that Susie was to be the Parade
Marshall this year and she was also being
honored by the state for her efforts at
preserving Brunswick County history. They
waved at each other as they passed and C.J.
called out "Hi, Miss Susie, are you ready for
the parade?"

"Hi, C.J., I am to ride on the antique fire truck,
you know. Always wanted to do that." They
smiled at each other and went their separate
ways. Everyone in town loved Miss Susie. She
was the cornerstone of the large Baptist
church on the corner a block away. Southport
Baptist Church would have been less of a
church without Miss Susie, Miss Margaret
McCracken, and Miss Annie Mae Woodside. It
was rather odd that three of the most well-
known elders of this church were all women.
That didn't happen much; especially in a

Southern Baptist Church. There were plenty of men of note in the church but these three ladies were all well known throughout the entire county and with the State Baptist Convention, as well. It was strange, though, that one church had three influential women in it who were well known county wide. Susie was even well known in the State offices and at Ridgecrest in the mountains. She even knew Billy and Ruth Graham.

C.J.'s cell phone rang. She hated the day the things had been invented. It was much more pleasant when phone calls were made on land lines and people had moments of peace and quiet when out walking. Now anyone could reach her anywhere. "Stone" she answered tersely. "Well, pull them apart, for Heaven's sake, and tell them to stop acting like children. Make certain they pay for the damage. No, I don't care if they say they hate each other; they always have. Just put them in the same car anyway. Maybe it will teach them a lesson in civility." Mayors! Something always happened right before the parade and it usually involved elected officials. This mayor didn't want to ride in a convertible. That mayor wanted to be in the first car. Another mayor thought he ought to be able to

AUTHOR: DIANNE WARTH-VEREEN

lead the parade. C.J. was tired of all the bickering between people who used to be rivals in basketball or football and had now grown up to be mayors of rival towns. Brunswick County was like a big family. Everyone knew each other and was related to each other in some connection along the way. They all fought the same way, too. It was just one big dysfunctional family. She went into Watson's Pharmacy and walked up to the soda fountain. "I'd like a vanilla Pepsi, please, Donnie," she said to the pre-pubescent boy who was the designated soda jerk for the morning. "Right away, Sheriff," he said. She sat down at one of the small metal tables and enjoyed the cool darkness of the interior of the building that never seemed to change. Locals walked by to the pharmacy in the back of the store to get their prescriptions filled by Dr. Willis or pick them up when done. Teens hung out at the front near the magazine racks trying to check out the girlie magazines on the top shelf before they were caught and told to go home. Southport; it never changed and there was nothing to compare with it.

The rest of the early morning was spent making sure that the town's decorations had been had been hung correctly and that the

AUTHOR: DIANNE WARTH-VEREEN

deputies all knew where they were going to be standing during the parade. The traffic patterns had all been drawn up, streets had been blocked off and C.J. felt certain that it wouldn't be too big a traffic jam with people coming in and out. She planned to route the outgoing traffic along Jabbertown Road and bring them out at the corner where 133 came to a stop near Hugh Spencer's gas station. The cars would be on the road to Wilmington and out of there before they could cause a traffic jam. At least the parade would be over before noon the next day and then she could relax and enjoy the rest of the festival. She never understood why the Sheriff was in charge of the parade and the Chief of Police was in charge of the rest of the festival. It was just one of those strange little Southport quirks. She spotted two more former schoolmates, Val and Barbara, and waved at them as she turned to walk toward the Courthouse and her office. It was going to be a hot day. She hoped that the parade would be unspoiled by rain and that it would all go perfectly.

The phone rang again and C.J. knew she was going to have a hard time with two of her former classmates. The two mayors and

AUTHOR: DIANNE WARTH-VEREEN

former school rivals were going to be a lot more trouble than they were worth. Why couldn't boys just grow up?

No one would have believed the thoughts of one former Southport High School student who was now Mayor of a local beach town. He was remembering his life in high school and the first years of college when he had been young, good looking and loaded with money. He thought about the phone call he had received from an old girlfriend who had acted as if they had been involved in the love affair of the Century. He didn't remember it that way; he remembered the young, perky blonde girl he had dated from Southport when he was home from college. She had been good looking and sweet but not the type of girl he would have married. His mother would never have approved of her. Still, they had dated for a while before she ran off after graduation to seek her fortune in the world of show biz. Why on Earth had she decided that she wanted to see him at this late date? She had acted like it was extremely important; a matter of life and death. Surely she couldn't be expecting him to still have feelings for her? Those had been gone five minutes after she left town.

The Fourth of July was always so hot that

AUTHOR: DIANNE WARTH-VEREEN

even a bathing suit was too much clothing.
The parade floats were lined up next to the
city garage and wiggled down the road beside
the hospital. They were colorful and inventive
and bore decorations from most of the area's
businesses. There were beauty queens from
every place in North and South Carolina. Even
Miss North Carolina and Miss Sun Fun from
Myrtle Beach were going to be in the parade.
One year Vanna White from Wheel of Fortune
won Miss Sun Fun. Several women were
milling around in long evening dresses waiting
for someone to help them up onto their floats.
One float had greenish, sparkly fish tails
tacked to the sides in which the girls could
hide their legs and instantly become
mermaids. It was going to be a good looking
float. Someone had spread builder's sand on
the top of the float to make it appear that the
children who were supposed to stand there
and ride the float looked like they were
playing on the beach. Someone had made
several sandcastles and they dotted the float
along with large plastic pails and colorful
canvas floats. There was always a lot of work
put into the floats. The 4th of July Parade was
very important to the state of North Carolina
and to Southport where it had been celebrated
longer than any other N.C. town.

AUTHOR: DIANNE WARTH-VEREEN

The parade cars were lined up back down the
road and the mayors and other "important
people" were finding their seats. Little Miss
Seashore pranced up and down near the car
she was going to ride in. She twirled a baton
with little flags attached to each end of the
twirling metal stick. There was one woman in
her 40's sitting on the back of a Corvette
wearing the shortest shorts ever seen on an
adult. The top that matched it was also a little
brief for an overly endowed woman but she
seemed to think she was beautiful and so did
her recently captured husband who was
driving the car. C.J. had to chuckle to herself
while thinking that some people wanted to be
seen whether or not anyone else wanted to see
them. It was funny what people would do for
attention; the two feuding mayors had just
realized that they were still supposed to be in
the same car. Neither one was very amused.
They were standing on either side of the car
waiting; not speaking to each other but
looking extremely aggravated about the
situation. When the signal had been given,
they each took a seat in the car but they were
trying very hard not to look at each other.
After fuming for a few seconds, the mayor
closest to the street got out and walked around
to look at the floats nearby leaving the other

AUTHOR: DIANNE WARTH-VEREEN

one in the car with the door open to get a little breeze. It seemed that he couldn't bear to even breathe the same air as his former friend.

Susie Carson was supposed to get on the fire truck to be in the parade. Susie had always loved fire trucks ever since she was a child. When she was about nine, her father had taken her to follow the fire truck every time the alarm sounded.

She realized her cat, Dudley, had followed her and she bent over to pick him up. Looking around, she found one of the children she knew from her Sunday school class and handed Dudley to him to take back to her house. "Make sure he stays there, too" said Susie and she went on her way to the fire house. Unfortunately, Dudley had a mind of his own and, as soon as Susie was out of sight, he jumped down from the boy's arms and ran through the park. The seven year old worried about it for about a minute before he spotted the hot dog cart and started worrying about if he had enough money to buy one. Everyone knew Dudley. The huge grey and white tom cat was famous for visiting people for a handout and then going back home to pretend he was starving. No one would hurt him and he would probably make it home on his own

AUTHOR: DIANNE WARTH-VEREEN

just fine. The cat melted into the shrubbery behind the firehouse. No doubt he smelled the hot dogs, too, and thought that someone might take pity on him and give him just a tiny little bite.

Different people commented on the loud arguments coming from the two feuding mayors before they had finally gotten into the car. There was a history between them that went back as far as grade school. The two had once been fast friends. They had played together as children and fished together as teens. Of course, a girl was what had come between them in high school. One mayor wanted the girl and the girl wanted the other mayor. Her name had been Margaret Anne and her long blonde hair, blue eyes and long slim body were the stuff of legends. Such feuds rarely go well and this one was no exception. Even now, thirty years later, the two sat together in the same car barely tolerating each other; rehashing old wounds loudly. At one point, the taller of the two made a threatening and obscene gesture to the other. "I swear one day I am going to kill you" yelled one of them at the other. The air in the car was so filled with vitriol and hate that the driver finally told them to shut up or get out. Instead of

AUTHOR: DIANNE WARTH-VEREEN

either of them doing so, the driver did. The car windows were rolled down and one door was slightly askew as they waited for the signal to start the engine and be ready. One mayor enjoyed his hot dog and then it looked like he dropped off to sleep with his hat down over his eyes and resting on his nose. The other mayor perched on the rear fender of the car and started to read a book he had brought. He would do anything not to have to endure his ex-friend's company. Susie's cat, Dudley, strolled nonchalantly over to the hospital front garden and sat there and licked his paws and cleaned his face. He had apparently just enjoyed a quick bite of lunch but no one seemed to notice. Deciding that no one was going to pick him up and cuddle him, he began his slow trek back to Moore Street and his cozy bed.

The parade was delayed thirty minutes (something that happened almost every year) but finally the cars and floats lined up to begin the trip down Howe Street toward the waterfront. C.J. Stone was still making her rounds to be certain all was well when she noticed that the car with the feuding mayors had not moved yet but was now very quiet. She knocked on the driver's side window and the driver rolled it down. "Awfully quiet in here," she nodded. "Why isn't he inside?" She nodded to the mayor sitting outside on the car. The driver turned around and spoke to the one on the fender. "Get in, "he said "you can't avoid him any longer. "He got in and slammed the door; hoping to wake up the other man. The mayor on the right side of the car seemed to be sound asleep but under his hat, his face had turned a strange shade of blue and one side of his mouth seemed to be drooping. C.J. motioned for the driver to pull the car over to the side of the street and let the rest of the parade go by them. Something was definitely wrong inside the car. The mayor who had stayed in the car the whole time didn't move and the other one opened the door and got out a lot faster than he had gotten in.

The driver was a paramedic so he leaped out of the driver's seat and ran around to the right side of the car to check the man who was slumped in the back seat. C.J. was on the phone calling for an ambulance to come from the fire station across the street but the other mayor was trying to drag his old nemesis from the car to get him laid flat on the ground. The driver was trying to get the Mayor to breathe. He had used his fingers to clear the airway

AUTHOR: DIANNE WARTH-VEREEN

and then, pinching the nose, breathed air into the Mayor's lungs through his mouth. A crowd gathered around and C.J. waved an officer over to disburse them. The parade was scheduled to start in just a few minutes. She asked the rival mayor if he remembered anything happening prior to them noticing that the other one seemed to be asleep. He said he hadn't because he had done his best to keep from noticing him at all the past fifteen years.

Mayor Tomkins was not asleep; he was **dead**. The paramedics loaded his body onto the gurney and pushed it up the slight hill to the hospital emergency room entrance. There was no reason to hurry anymore. He wouldn't be able to ride in the parade. Mayor Bentley would have to ride in another car alone. There was no reason to get everyone all worked up and spoil the parade. He was dead and there was nothing they could do about it. The officers were told to have the car dusted for prints and checked out from top to bottom. Someone called a wrecker to come up the back road and tow the car to the police impound lot after forensics had time to finish. C.J. called the coroner and told him to head to the ER to check out the body. She wanted to know if

AUTHOR: DIANNE WARTH-VEREEN

there were any marks that suggested foul play. What a way to start the 4th of July Parade. The colors flying from each float and on the buildings on the parade route reminded everyone how proud they were of their country's heritage. Each year the locals welcomes thousands of guests to their small town to celebrate like they had for many decades. Each year was better than the last one.

She had someone take Bentley's statement and told him to go to the station after the parade to see if he was needed for anything else. Since he had been out of the car the whole time it was doubtful he had seen anything. Finally she shoved him into the back seat of a dune buggy which was the last car available since the rest had been taken up by beauty queens and the one he was supposed to be in was now a piece of police evidence. He took the opportunity to divest himself of suit coat and tie and open his shirt and roll up the sleeves. Unlike Tomkins who wore a suit for everyday, Bentley hated them and took every chance to not wear one. Someone handed him an old Southport High School ball cap and he slapped it on top of his head and put on his sunglasses. He was good to go.

The bands were all lined up and had started tuning up their instruments all at the same time with the result of a sound that was indescribable. Everyone was scrambling up onto the floats and getting into their places. The little children that were in the parade were all taking their final turns in the Porta-Potties that were placed nearby. The line was a long one and wound down the road that passed the ER side of the hospital. At the very end of the line was the old fashioned fire truck that Mr. Hubbard had owned and J.B. and Terry had restored to perfection for display at the Fire Department. Someone was helping Miss Susie climb up a step ladder onto the truck where she seated herself with a kind of dignity that only she could have while wearing a huge white sun hat crowned with a red-white-and –blue ribbon that dangled down the back. She wore another of her daughter Kathryn's creations; a bright red pants suit with patriotic buttons and belt. At the last minute one of the kids saw Dudley and handed him to Susie on the fire truck. Dudley enjoyed the ride as far as Hufham's Exxon and then hopped down and ran away when the fire truck slowed to a short stop on the parade

AUTHOR: DIANNE WARTH–VEREEN

route.

The people that crowded the sidewalks were from everywhere. They had brought children and grandchildren, friends and neighbors to the parade that took place every year. The Arts and Crafts show was on its final day. The park was filled with small booths and tables with locally and N.C. made crafts and the big art display over near the City Hall building.

As the bands played and the floats passed, the children cheered and waved. Everyone loves the 4th of July parade. Little kids were running beside the fire truck calling "Miss Susie; Miss Susie." Others were begging for candy and beads and other "throw aways" that were flying from the floats to the onlookers on the side of the streets. Everyone turned out; no matter how hot it was. The inviting scents from the various street vendors' carts were making everyone hungry. Children were enjoying shaved ice cones in paper cups that were covered in bright, staining colors. Ice cream melted on shirts and fingers. Hot dogs were devoured while the parade passed by.

The sidewalks were lined with people three and four deep. It was almost impossible to walk anyplace. Kids were sitting on the curbs and a lot of the people were waving American flags. The town had been decorated with red-white-and-blue bunting and huge bows hung on the doors of the little shops that lined the parade route. Clowns rode little tiny bicycles and unicycles and weaved in and out between the floats, cars and bands. Babies in strollers alternately cried and laughed. Adults got hot as the July sun beamed down on their heads. A television station from Wilmington had set up its cameras on the corner of Howe and Moore where the viewing stands had been built for the dignitaries who had been especially invited. Everyone would be watching their video recorders and the news later to see if they could find themselves in the crowd.

Everyone was having a wonderful time. The music was made up mostly of John Philip Sousa's marches with a few songs that were meant to inspire national pride thrown in. A band from a middle school in Wilmington was murdering "God Bless America" but the parents seemed to think it was great. The Dunn Clowns' jail car went by crowded with several local school teachers who were being held for ransom. They held signs out through the bars that said "Help me get out of jail.

Contribute $1.00". It was doubtful they would be released before dark.

One of the banks was throwing chocolate candy that looked like gold coins. The kids loved them but the adults would have preferred the real thing. A real estate float was covered with sand that was so hot that the girls kept moving from one foot to the other. It would have been hard not to notice that the girl in the patriotic two piece bathing suit was turning bright pink. Obviously she had forgotten her sun screen or needed another coat slathered on.

The bands and floats followed each other until finally the bright red fire truck came rolling down Moore street. Miss Susie was smiling and waving at everyone. She had taught a lot of them in Sunday school and they still remembered her and loved her. The older people waving at her were either her Sunday school kids grown up or members of her genealogy class. She was the perfect parade marshal.

As the fire truck turned the corner to drive up Moore Street people on Howe Street started to disburse. The kids ran up Moore Street to see Miss Susie and see if they could get a ride on the antique fire truck, too.

C.J. was glad the parade was almost over so that she could talk to the Coroner and the Southport Police Chief about their dead Mayor. She couldn't help but think something strange was going on. Hadn't Tomkins seemed perfectly alright just an hour before she found him dead? Surely he hadn't died just from breathing the same air as Bentley. That was taking dislike a little too far even for an X-file.

Kathryn walked up to help her mother alight from the fire truck. She had sworn never to come home for the Fourth of July because she hated the heat but what could she do when her mother was being honored? She had been chosen to be parade marshal and tonight she would be getting a special award. She helped her down from the truck and tucked her into her car for a short trip to a friend's house for lunch. She wore a floppy white straw hat and a navy blue pants suit that she had made a week before her arrival.

"Dudley finally showed up a little while ago, Mama," she said to Susie. "The littlest Faulk boy brought him home. He said he found him in the park at the hot dog stand begging for scraps." They both laughed. Dudley was

AUTHOR: DIANNE WARTH-VEREEN

famous for his appetite and his ability to forget he was a cat and beg like a dog.

"I thought he was safely at home," answered Susie. "Sometimes he baffles me how he gets out of the house without anyone knowing." She removed her huge sun hat and combed her hair in the car mirror. "How did I look on the fire truck? It was so much fun, you know. Daddy used to take us every time the fire siren went off. I have always loved fire trucks. It was a real honor to be able to ride with the Chief. I am so glad they picked me to be the marshal."

"The real honor is tonight at the dinner," said Kathryn. "You are getting an award as the town's official historian. I have it in confidence that one of your favorite people is catering the dinner; Quack Sanders. I wonder what he has thought up for you." Susie smiled. Quack's daughter, Nancy, had been in Susie's Sunday school class and also been Kathryn's classmate in school. She had often stopped by after school for one of Big Mama's biscuits with jam. Big Mama had been Kathryn's name for grandmother. The thought of perfectly fried local shrimp and crab cakes filled Susie's thoughts on the short ride.

AUTHOR: DIANNE WARTH-VEREEN

Everyone knew Quack. He had been the school principal, math teacher, coach and also owned and operated a wonderful seafood restaurant down at the old Yacht Basin called Quack's Sea Shack. His seafood was always fresh from the local boats and he always employed great local cooks. Kathryn's mouth was watering just thinking about it all. One year he had been the senior class advisor and had actually roasted a pig and provided the food for a full South Seas luau for the senior prom. She knew that he had something very special planned for her mother's dinner.

The dinner in Susie's honor was to be held at the Community Building on the waterfront at the Garrison. During the Second World War, it had been used as the U.S.O. and Susie had met her husband there while he was in the Army. She had been serving donuts to the soldiers and sailors on a Friday night as she usually did when he came in with a friend. She had enjoyed her turns as a "donut dolly" and had kept a large scrap book about the town during the war. It might have been what got her started on being the town's historian. Over the years, she had written several books about the founding and growth of the town, the oldest cemetery in town (which was just up the street from her house) and about various people she had known during her life. She had helped found the Southport Historical Society and recently had become a teacher at the Community College where she taught classes on local genealogy. Now Susie was renown all over the South for her genealogy and history work. Indeed, she was proud to be honored in her hometown.

Two

"Kathryn, can you help me get into this outfit?" She gestured toward the long white robe that had been sent over that afternoon for her to wear to the presentation before the dinner. "Why on earth do you suppose they want me to wear this thing? It is just going to be too hot in that building with all those people. This thing looks like our choir robes." Susie fumed as Kathryn lowered the robe over her head and settled it around her shoulders to hang correctly.

"Well," Kathryn said soothingly. "Don't you look nice? Let's get a picture of you. You look like you are graduating from high school all over again. All you need is a mortar board hat." She took a quick photo of her mother, picked up her purse and escorted her out the door to the car. "We just have to swing by and pick up Miss Annie Mae, "Kathryn said as they started off down the street. Miss Annie Mae Woodside had the designation as the first female superintendent of schools for Brunswick County. She lived alone in a big old house on the waterfront just down the street from Susie's. Her closest neighbors were a Superior court judge and a local surgeon. To pick her up, Kathryn drove her car through a small alley that seemed to be covered by the trees and bushes that grew on either side. Two outside cats stood guard by the garden. The door opened in a few minutes and Miss Annie Mae joined them for the trip to the Garrison and Susie's award du jour.

When they all arrived at the Community Building, they were surprised at how many people were already there standing outside near the wooden stage that had been erected. Apparently, part of the honors was to be held outside so that anyone who wanted to attend could. One of the local ministers stepped forward to guide Susie up to take her place of honor. A young man she had taught in Sunday

AUTHOR: DIANNE WARTH-VEREEN

school stepped forward and placed a graduation cap on her head. A young woman she had once mentored in G.A.s dropped a wide ribbon over her head and across her chest. The local school band began to play the poignant song "It's May the month of Roses" which was always played in Southport on class night before the high school graduation. Everyone in the crowd calmed down and became silent. Susie was wondering what was going to happen next. Tugg Bentley, Mayor of Southport, stepped up to introduce a local area man who was also a State Senator. He asked that Susie step forward and then made a speech presenting her with a certificate saying she was being recognized as the official Southport Historian by the State of North Carolina. He presented her with a plaque that said just that. Then someone from the Chancellor's office at the county Community College said he was there to give her an honorary college degree for all of her work in the areas of local genealogy and local history. "Well, that explains the cap and gown," she said with a big smile as the man flipped the tassel on the graduation cap to the "graduated" position. A photographer from the local paper took lots of pictures and promised to give Kathryn one for her mother's scrap

AUTHOR: DIANNE WARTH-VEREEN

book. The band played a couple of patriotic songs and then the invited guests filed into the Community Building for the dinner in Susie's honor.

The Community Building had long been used for junior-senior banquets for the local high school so no one was expecting anything spectacular. They were surprised to see a large dais set up at the back of the room holding the head table. The other people were seated at smaller tables of six spread out in the room. A small group of local musicians was playing on a small stage near the French doors that led to the porch.

In her place of honor at the head of the table on the dais, Susie looked around at the people who were at the different tables. "Where is Harry Tomkins?" Susie turned to ask one of the people sitting next to her. His seat and that of his current wife were both empty. All of the local Mayors were supposed to be sitting at the head table. Tomkins was conspicuous by his absence.

"Didn't you hear?" whispered Ally Kimble who was just beginning to serve the head table their drinks. "Mr. Tomkins was found dead just as the parade started." Ally was a senior at the local high school. She had always been one of Susie's favorite young ladies but the words that came from her lips shocked her just the same. "**DEAD**?" Susie shrieked. "How on earth could he have been found dead? I saw him earlier and he was just fine as frog hair. He was just in his 50's. My goodness, his daddy must be heartbroken." She remembered Harry Tomkins from when he was just a child in her Sunday school class at the Baptist Church. "Will someone tell me what happened?"

C.J. Stone was also at the head table and she stood up to talk to the room filled with Southport people. "Everyone here has probably heard about the death of Harry Tomkins this morning just before the parade. He was found dead in the car he was supposed to ride in with Mayor Bentley. He appeared to be asleep but he had no pulse and had stopped breathing. His body has been flown to Chapel Hill for a full autopsy to see if they can figure out what happened. There was no evidence at the crime scene of foul play. He had no marks on his body to indicate that he had been harmed with any sort of weapon or even poisoned." There was a gasp as Stone mentioned poison and weapons. Who had ever

AUTHOR: DIANNE WARTH-VEREEN

heard of such things in Southport? "We are asking everyone who saw Harry to cooperate with the local police department and my deputies to see if we can find any clues to what happened. We just can't allow a stain on the good name of our town. "She started to sit down and then turned back around "Our sympathies are with his family for his passing." She sat down in her chair and had a big gulp of water from the large goblet at her left hand. She couldn't believe her luck. Here she was, the first woman sheriff in Brunswick County and only 6 months into her job the mayor of one of the beach communities dies right out in public on the Fourth of July. It was rotten luck. She just hoped she could solve the crime quickly and then forget about it.

As the food was served everyone was talking about the death at the parade and wondering what could possibly have happened. This Fourth of July was truly turning out to be murder!

Sparkie Mills was a hometown girl who had made good. She was currently starring in the lounge at Caesar's in Las Vegas. It had been an effort but C.J. had talked her into finagling

AUTHOR: DIANNE WARTH-VEREEN

a little time off over the 4th to sing at Susie's
dinner and perform at the festival on the
waterfront stage. Long gone from Southport,
Sparkie had been surprised when she had first
come home for her only visit since she'd hit the
road west. Not a lot had changed. Oh yeah,
there were fast food places and a Wal-Mart
but the waterfront was much the same and
the Yacht Basin was still there. She smoothed
her hands on the skirt of her tight white
sheath dress as the Mayor introduced her to
the group. The band began to play "Smoke
Gets in Your Eyes" and Sparkie walked onto
the stage to huge applause. She smiled at the
people she knew that were there and sort of
overlooked the others who were there because
they were students of Miss Susie's or members
of the Historical Society. When she grabbed
the microphone and started to sing you could
have heard a pin drop. Sparkie had real talent
and it showed. She did a set with five songs
from the 50's and then walked over to the
head table to kiss Susie on the cheek and
whisper in C.J.'s ear "I 'll see you back at the
house, okay?" Then she walked out onto the
porch that surrounded the building. She
stared out at the Cape Fear River and listened
to the sounds of the band at the Cedar Bench
playing for the young people who were

AUTHOR: DIANNE WARTH-VEREEN

gathered to listen to the music and dance the shag. The music was the slow easy rhythm that always made a shagger's feet move even if he were sitting still. She decided to walk toward the music she could hear from the waterfront and reached down to take off her shoes. She hated wearing high heels in the summer time. Her feet always wanted to swell and then her shoes pinched. She walked in the slow sauntering way she had always had. Even though it was night there was enough light from the music areas to let her see where the road dropped off on one side onto the beach below. She moved herself out into the center of the road as a car slowed down. A guy she hadn't seen in years leaned out of the car and said "I'd know that swing anywhere! Hello, Sparkie. When did you get back in town?"

Jim Earl Dean was the last person in the world that Sparkie Mills ever wanted to see again. The desire to turn and go the other direction was strong but Sparkie made herself stand and talk to him civilly. He probably didn't even remember the last time they had seen each other. There had just been the three of them at the Cedar Bench that night. Sparkie, Jim Earl and Harry Tomkins. Ten

AUTHOR: DIANNE WARTH-VEREEN

o'clock on a Friday night and none of them had any place to be except in a car circling the Cedar Bench. Sparkie had just broken up with her boyfriend of three years, Woody Hart. Jim Earl was drunk; as usual. Harry Tomkins had been doing what he did best; trying to impress other people. It had been a long time ago. The past was past. Jim Earl crawled along in his car beside Sparkie as she walked toward the music. It was obvious he thought he might be able to start up a little something but Sparkie had other plans. She wasn't sticking around after the 4th. Thomas Wolfe had been right when he said "you can't go home again." No matter how big you made it someplace else you were always the same person in your home town that you were when you left. She let out her breath as they reached the parking area at the edge of the waterfront park. It was roped off and once she stepped past the rope Jim Earl couldn't follow her unless he got out and walked. He didn't and she felt relief. She could make it just two more days and once she got on that plane back to Vegas she wasn't ever coming back.

"Miss Grace" had just started to play on the bandstand when Sparkie finally made it to the center of all the fun. This was her kind of

AUTHOR: DIANNE WARTH-VEREEN

crowd not the historical types at the dinner. She breathed in the salty air and the seafood scents from Mack's Café. Home; it was a place she hadn't thought about seriously in a very long time. When C.J. had called and asked her to come for the N.C. Fourth of July Festival, she had thought it was a good chance to reconnect with her hometown. She had already been to the cemetery to pay homage to her parents and sister. She had spent lots of time with C.J. and her husband. She had seen the Post Office that had been built near the site of the old high school. She had walked around down town and visited all the little shops that stood where the old bus station used to be and the appliance shop had once stood. She had run into a few of the people she had liked in high school and some she hadn't. Her parent's old house was now a B & B called Capt. Hook's. She had eaten lunch there the previous day. The traffic was just too horrible to take her rental convertible and drive over to the beaches. Things definitely weren't going the way she had planned.

Sparkie walked away from the bandstand and sat down on one of the swings at the edge of the water. She looked out over the river at the reflections of all the beautiful lights from

Caswell and the beach. In the distance there were pretty colors on Bald Head Island. Everyone was celebrating the 4th. She thought about the people who had been close to her when she was in high school. What had she really expected? Did she truly think she could just waltz back into his life after ten years? Did she expect time to stop for them and begin again when she arrived in Southport? She should have expected it. Nothing ever went the way she expected; why should now be any different? She should never have come. How had she let C.J. talk herself into coming back even for just a few days? Some boxes were made to never be opened.

Three

"I still don't understand why you think you have to leave this morning, Sparkie." C.J. Stone had just tumbled out of bed. Her prematurely silver hair was tousled badly and she was dressed in her pink bunny slippers and old quilted bathrobe she had owned since her first son was born. "I thought you were going to stay for a week, at least."

Sparkie Mills paced the small kitchen with a

worried look on her face. Her curly blonde hair was pulled into a pony tail like she had worn it in high school. "I have to go, C.J. I just can't stand it here anymore."

"What happened?" asked C.J.'s husband as he walked into the room. "You   seemed to be having a pretty good time yesterday. Why did you change your mind?" He helped himself to a big cup of coffee and a piece of the crisp bacon C.J. had just fried. "Aren't you having fun seeing all of your old friends?"

"No; I am not. Southport isn't like I remember it. I went into Mack's yesterday to get some hush puppies and sweet tea and there were **boys** waiting on tables there. I remember Miss Lillian Collins and Miss Betty taking orders. Once in a while one of the local girls would fill in. Boys don't belong waiting on tables. The one who waited on me told me that hush puppies came with a meal and I couldn't just order six of them and a glass of tea. I just got up and left. Later on, I went in Watson's for a vanilla Pepsi and the girl behind the counter looked at me like I had three heads. What is with these people? Even at the dinner last night I didn't feel comfortable. I saw Binky Webb and he acted like he didn't even know me. I changed his diapers when he was a

AUTHOR: DIANNE WARTH-VEREEN

baby, for Heaven's sake!"

"Your leaving wouldn't have anything to do with the death of Harry Tomkins, would it?" C.J. was one of the few people who could remember that Sparkie had once had a terrible crush on the town's badly behaved rich boy.

"Of course not" Sparkie answered much too quickly to suit C.J.

"Well, I am sure if I need you for the trial or to answer any questions I can find you easily enough. Still, you won't be able to get a plane back to Vegas till all the tourists leave. The airlines are fully booked. I checked as soon as you mentioned you were thinking about leaving."

"An airplane isn't the only way out of this town," said Sparkie. "I'll just drive to Raleigh or Charlotte and take a plane from there. Can I use your computer to find a flight?"

"I guess so," answered C.J. "but couldn't you stay at least until the end of the festival? I thought you were supposed to sing at the show right before the fireworks."

"I was but I called Butchie Brenner last night

AUTHOR: DIANNE WARTH-VEREEN

and told her something had come up and I had to go back to the west coast. The crowning of Miss 4th of July will just have to go on without my singing that rendition of "Miss 4th of July" that Ms. Leila wrote to be sung to that Miss America theme that Bert Parks used to sing. They can get someone else to sing it or do without it all together. I don't care; I just want to get out of here."

"I thought you wanted me to teach you how to play that ukulele you bought at the flea market," piped up C.J.'s husband. "You've only had one lesson."

"Keep it. Your granddaughter can learn to play it." Everything they said to try to convince Sparkie to stay just made her more determined to leave as soon as possible. "I'm hitting the road as soon as I find a flight and know where I have to go to catch it." She walked out onto the front porch and watched as some kids rode their bikes past the house toward the festival area.

"Something weird is going on with Sparkie, "whispered C.J. to her husband. " She was so excited when she was planning to come. "Something happened yesterday. I'd bet my badge on that!" She wiped her hands on the apron that covered her uniform. Just as she was about to make another remark the telephone rang and work was calling.

"Sheriff, the slice and dice in Chapel Hill is over. They didn't find any evidence of foul play. There was no poison in the blood, no wounds on the body, no alcohol or drugs present in the tox screen. The medical examiner is baffled. He has called New Hanover and Dosher for any medical histories they might have had on hand for Tomkins. Dr. Patel is taking his records from his office and picking up the hospital records at both hospitals. Then he is going up to Chapel Hill to see if he can help figure it out. It's like he just sat down and died."

C.J. hung up the receiver and looked out at her friend standing on the porch. Something was up with Sparky and it had something to do with Harry Tomkins or she hadn't read every Nancy Drew book ever written as a kid.

Four

"I am glad Mr. Prevatte gave me a few days

off, Susie said to her daughter. "I usually don't get to spend enough time with you when you are home." They were in Kathryn's little white Volkswagen on the way to see Minnie Rivers over on Long Beach. "Has Minnie ever met Arnold, Kathryn? I can't seem to remember."

"Yes, Mama, she met him right after we got married. They get along really well. Arnold has so many science fiction books and magazines that Arnold feels right at home. She is planning to cook supper for all of us when he gets here. Did I tell you he found a Maine Coon cat at the rescue center and he is bringing it to her to replace the one she had?"

"Does she know?"

"No, it's a surprise. It will be alright, though, because I know she has been looking for one. They are so expensive to buy and this one is not even a year old so it will be easy for them to bond to each other."

They rode down beach road toward the Inland Waterway. Traffic was thick coming from the beach toward Southport and they had to slow down to less than 25 miles per hour several times. People had decorated their property

AUTHOR: DIANNE WARTH-VEREEN

and houses for the national holiday. Red,
white and blue ribbons and bows hung on
doors and flags flew everywhere. They
stopped for a few minutes to run into the
Salvation Army Thrift Store and see what was
new. After buying several hard backed books
they returned to the car to finish their trip. By
the time they reached the waterway bridge,
they were both eager to finish their drive.

They pulled into the circular drive at their
friend's house and she met them at the door
with a smile. Right behind them, Arnold
pulled up in his rented pickup with the kitty
he had rescued from the pound.

"Oh, he's so beautiful," said Minnie as she took
the cat and started petting him. "Thank you,
Arnold!"

They all went into the living room of the
house and the cat began to jump up on   the
furniture. "Have you heard any more about
Harry Tomkins' death? It sure sounds weird to
me." Susie asked Minnie since Tomkins had
been Mayor of Yaupon Beach.

"Well, everyone knew that he and Bentley
hated each other. There's been a lot of talk
about that. There has been some talk about

AUTHOR: DIANNE WARTH-VEREEN

his wives (or should I say ex-wives). They didn't seem to like him much once they weren't married to him. He had three or four; not counting the one he married in April. He had some enemies from his days in Washington as the aid to that Senator, too," said Minnie.

"Well, according to C.J., there were no toxins found in the body. There were no marks found on the body, either. We have to assume that the death was caused by something 'natural'." Kathryn spoke the words she and her mother had already discussed on the trip to the beach. "We just have to figure out what that was."

The telephone rang in the other room and Minnie got up to go answer it. "One of my renters called to see if the street dance in Southport had been cancelled because of Tomkins's death." Everyone laughed at the question. "As if the dance depended on Tomkins existence. Anyway, as you were saying, he had enemies and exes so a lot of people could have killed him. How did they do it?"

Susie finished her cup of tea and then said "I never trust a man who doesn't like cats."

AUTHOR: DIANNE WARTH-VEREEN

"What?" Arnold had tried to follow the conversation so far but had found it more than difficult. "Who doesn't like cats? I thought everybody here liked cats."

"Oh, everyone here does like cats. Harry Tomkins didn't though. That's why I never liked him. When he was a little boy he snuck into my backyard after kindergarten was over one day and tied a rasher of bacon to the tails of my two cats with twine. All of the neighborhood dogs chased them all the way down to the waterfront where your granddaddy's store was. He said they were so tired they just flopped down onto the floor when he got them free from the twine. That's all that was left. The bacon was all gone and so was the end of Tippy's tail. When I faced his mother with this all she did was laugh and say, 'boys will be boys'. She didn't even punish him."

Everyone sat there dumbfounded. "Gosh," said Minnie, "If he was so mean to animals when he was a kid that he might have been mean to someone who decided to get back at him. "

"Yeah, but who could it have been?" Arnold asked.

AUTHOR: DIANNE WARTH-VEREEN

"Well, that's what we have to figure out," answered Kathryn. "Let's make a list of all of his friends and then one of his enemies, too. Wonder what C.J. has found out. Why don't you give her a call, Minnie? You and she were in the same class in school, maybe she will tell you something she wouldn't normally tell anyone."

{ On the phone}

"No, there haven't been any developments in the case," said C.J. "I wish something would turn up. I can't seem to find out anything that could help. I have talked to the ex-wives and the ex-girlfriends, and his former employer and his Washington associates. They all swear that they haven't even talked to Harry lately. One of his ex-wives said it couldn't have happened to a nicer person. "C.J. laughed a little as she said it. "There are some people left in Washington to talk to but I don't think we are getting anywhere. The only person I haven't talked to is Sparkie."

"Sparkie? Why on earth would you want to talk to Sparkie? She hasn't been in Southport for years until she came to sing at Susie's dinner."

AUTHOR: DIANNE WARTH-VEREEN

"Geez, have you forgotten? I thought you remembered everything." C.J. sounded a little disappointed in her friend. Minnie was supposed to remember everything!

"What have I forgotten? Sparkie Mills was four classes behind us. She left here about three hours after graduation. I was away at ECU then. She was always popular. She was beautiful and talented and she was just 13 when we graduated and I went off to college. I barely knew anything about her."

"I forgot. Ok, here's the story. Sparkie was the prettiest girl in the freshman class. Harry Tomkins was, well, he was Harry Tomkins! Junior class president, captain of the football team, forward on the basketball team, rich and good looking. Sparkie lived with her mother in that house on the waterfront. Her mother rented out rooms to school teachers and people who were only in town for a little while. Sparkie had the biggest crush on him in the world. She and my sister Angie were friends so I saw her quite a lot. We became friends, too, and she often told me that she would give anything to go out with Harry. "

"Okay, so what's the big deal? I doubt she killed him because she had a crush on him and he didn't return the favor."

"No, but that isn't exactly what happened. Harry pretty much ignored her until after he graduated and went off to college. He only stayed at State for two years. The second year he came home at Christmas and didn't go back. That's when he noticed Sparkie. She was even more beautiful then than she had been in high school. She was getting ready to graduate and go on to college when that Christmas Harry Tomkins asked her to be his date to the yearly Woman's Club Christmas dance that was held at the Community building. She was so excited. I went with her to Raleigh just to find the perfect dress to wear. I know she must have saved for weeks to be able to buy it. I was already there that night when they came in. Harry looked great, as usual, and Sparkie was beautiful. They were the hit of the dance. They looked like the perfect couple. They danced as if they had been made for each other. Harry looked at her like she was the only person in the room. I thought it was love. Boy was I wrong."

"I didn't come home in time for that dance. I went to Annapolis for that week to see the guy I was dating. What happened? I know there has to be more to this story."

AUTHOR: DIANNE WARTH-VEREEN

"I don't know the whole story. I just know that just as fast as it began it was over. Sparkie stopped coming around to see me and her and Angie stopped hanging out together. Right after graduation in May she left Southport and never came back again until this week."

"So how did y'all start talking to each other again?"

"Remember when her Aunt Caroline was in that wreck and was paralyzed? Sparkie called me and asked me to go by and check on her and let her know how she really was. We started calling each other regularly and our friendship started up again. We have talked to each other once a week ever since then. We have met up several times on vacations. I have gone out to Vegas to see her three times and we have met in Cabo San Lucas on vacation at least five times. It was really difficult to get her to come home for this week. When she finally agreed she asked me if I thought she would run into Harry. Like an idiot, I said no. I can't say for sure that she did but I can't think of any other reason she would have left the day after Susie's award ceremony."

"Well, something happened to Harry because he's dead. We have to figure out what it was."

AUTHOR: DIANNE WARTH-VEREEN

Dianne paused to think and C.J. took the opportunity to make a remark.

"Yes, he is, Minnie, but **we** do not have to figure out why. The autopsy in Chapel Hill didn't turn up anything that our coroner didn't notice when he did his. I don't think there is a magic answer to find. Let the professionals do their job and stop trying to be Nancy Drew."

"Ha! As if! I couldn't care less who 'offed' Harry." said Minnie "Still, an outside set of eyes and another mind or two won't hurt anything. If I come up with anything I will let you know. "

"Yeah, you do that," she laughed. "If you figure it out before the professionals do, I will take you out to eat anyplace you want to go, Nancy Drew!"

The phone call ended with a big laugh and Minnie came back into the room where her friends were all still talking about the strange death of Harry Tomkins. Their visit was one of conviviality and deep friendship. The cat seemed to be adjusting to her new home and Susie was in her element with her "children" all around her.

Life had not always treated Susie as a favored

child; despite what most people thought. She had been a popular girl in school and had never lacked for friends or dates. Her sister, Thelma, and she were very close to their brother, William. The family was large; sometimes it felt like they were related to everyone in Brunswick County. Cousins saw each other often as family gatherings occurred several times per year. No one thought Susie would ever leave Brunswick County but after meeting an interesting stranger one Friday night at the U.S.O., that's exactly what she did.

She had married a young man who was in the Army and moved with him to Washington, D.C. Having spent her entire life in Brunswick County, she had not adjusted well to life in the nation's capital but she had tried to be what she perceived was a good Army wife. It was difficult for her to be away from her family and friends but she seemed to manage well until she found out she was going to have a baby. That was when she decided she had to return to Brunswick County and she had been there, except for a few trips to neighboring states, ever since.

In the end, she had remained in the home of her parents and raised her child alone. Her

AUTHOR: DIANNE WARTH-VEREEN

army husband stayed in Washington; coming
to Southport ever so often for a short visit.
Married but on her own, she learned how to
take care of herself and struggled to provide a
home without him. Eventually, in order to
purchase property in her own name, she went
against her conscience and beliefs and
obtained a divorce from the good looking man
who had stolen her heart. He later moved on
and married someone else. Believing that
marriage is forever between a couple, Susie
never remarried. She managed to establish
her own credit which was unheard of for a
woman in the early 50's. She worked for
lawyers as a legal secretary but she absorbed
as much about the legal system as if she had
been a university student seeking a law
degree. People trusted Susie and identified
with her. She became the most well known
woman in the county and, in her own quiet
way, took the first steps toward female
emancipation and identity. At a time when
women were identified with their husband or
parents, she established herself as a force to
reckon with. Her judgment was considered
impeccable and it was just normal that the
case of Harry Tomkins's widow came to rest on
her desk within a day of the family's
discussion about his death.

AUTHOR: DIANNE WARTH-VEREEN

"Susie," said Mr. Prevatte as he laid a thick folder on her desk. "I can't make heads nor tails of this whole thing. Harry's widow wants me to ask the judge to allow her to dispose of all their joint assets at once without waiting until the normal time for probate to be achieved. She has listed nearly every thing that is in their joint names and signed statements that it was all originally in her name alone. She claims his name was added over a month after they were married (without her permission) and that she (and she alone) paid for all of the items. She is claiming that no one that can claim kinship to Harry is entitled to any of the property and that his estate has to be considered without the property. She plans to get rid of everything immediately.

This list here is supposed to be what Harry actually owned in his own name at the time of their marriage. It just includes that 60' boat that's docked in the boat harbor and the jeep that he kept parked at the dock. According to these papers, she owned everything else when they got married. Even the jaguar, which she has already made arrangements to sell, was in her name prior to their marriage. Do you have Harry's file from when we drew up his

AUTHOR: DIANNE WARTH-VEREEN

prenuptial agreement? We have to have everything matched up before we appear in Judge Bellamy's courtroom for the hearing tomorrow. "

Susie ran through the index of papers that she had gathered and checked to see that all was in order. It was unusual for a widow to petition the court to set aside probate on the grounds that the widow had paid for all of the property herself prior to the marriage. Harry Tomkins life had been one giant mess and Susie didn't like meddling in it even if he was dead.

She looked at the list of phone calls with claims to the estate. All of his former wives were claiming that they were entitled to a portion of the estate even after their settlements had been paid out. It was a good thing Harry had never sired any children. They would have been very disappointed in the type of man their father had been.

She called Jimmy Goodnight and asked him to take a list of property transfers over to the Register of Deeds and check to make certain that the widow spoke the truth. If Harry hadn't really owned anything there were going to be some upset people who weren't going to get paid for his debts. It was certainly beginning to look like Harry Tomkins had been a Class A deadbeat. She called Kathryn and told her what was going on and that she might be late getting back to the house. Her daughter reported that Dudley had again managed to sneak out of the house and was wandering around without supervision. Knowing that one of her former Sunday school students would find him and return him to her home, she went on with her work without giving it a second thought.

Five

July was hotter than ever before in the history of recorded temperatures in the area. The tourists seemed to be spending less time in the ocean and that was probably because the water was so hot that it was driving the fish in closer to the shore. People were reporting bites by blue fish that seemed to be thrusting their sharp little teeth into tender feet several times per week. Luckily there hadn't been any jelly fish stings reported.

The beaches were packed with brightly colored bathing suits and beach towels. Some people

AUTHOR: DIANNE WARTH-VEREEN

were bringing large beach umbrellas to keep
them cooler in the middle of the day. The local
stores were restocking their sun block more
often. Coolers were being filled with ice and
bottled water to be consumed during the day.
No matter the temperature, people baked on
the strand covered in Coppertone or Iodine
and Baby oil.

Harry Tomkins' widow had put their home up
for sale. The house, which was at the far end
of the island, had been built in the late sixties
and was one of the first multiple family homes
that were called family vacation compounds. It
was right on the waterway and had a long
dock at which was moored a nice boat. She
hadn't wanted to buy the house but Harry had
insisted that it was perfect for them and
whined about it until she had agreed. It didn't
hold any sentimental value for her. She
considered it a big money pit and hoped to
collect a small fortune from its sale. She had
already made plans to sell Harry's Porsche
convertible and his motorcycle. His parents
were dismayed at how fast she seemed to be
getting over their son's death. She was already
planning to move back to Charlotte and had
been driving back and forth for the last two
weeks to find a place to live and a job. Like his

AUTHOR: DIANNE WARTH-VEREEN

parents, some local people were still hoping for an explanation for his sudden death. Fifteen days had already passed with no clue as to what had happened.

Susie Carson had gone back to work on the 10th of July. Her daughter and she had spent most of the 4th of July vacation going places and seeing people they hadn't seen in a while. She had really enjoyed her daughter and son-in-law's visit this time. Usually she was working when they were in Southport but she had taken her vacation time and enjoyed every day they had been able to stay. She had been busy with a big land case that Mr. Prevatte was handling and she was learning a lot about how the land in Brunswick County had changed hands over the years. She had been surprised to discover that one law about inheritance had not changed until after the 1950's. This law was important because it decreed that property owned by a husband did not necessarily pass to the wife at the husband's death. It all depended on how the husband came by the property in the first place. For instance, if a husband inherited property at his wife's death and then remarried, the second wife would actually not have a claim to that property at his death

AUTHOR: DIANNE WARTH-VEREEN

unless a will were made that so designated the passage of that property being signed by all other heirs. This would sure have complicated the inheritance laws of the county since most of the widowed men remarried within the first year after their wife's death. The case they were working on was one of those cases. Tom Gray had died. His second wife, Penelope, was claiming title to all of the land he had owned. She had been planning to parcel it out among her step-children and her own children in a will. Two of the deceased's children were contesting Penelope's claim to the land on the grounds that it had actually belonged to their deceased mother (having been inherited at the death of her father).It looked to be a big battle in the courts. Susie had felt some empathy for Penelope at the beginning of the case but then had heard stories about the circumstances of the marriage and decided that the new widow might have married Tom Gray because of his land holdings and income from that land. The law was interesting. Brunswick County was one of the most interesting counties in North Carolina. It was the largest county in land mass. It has the dubious honor of being the 37th fastest growing county in the United States. Not that any of this pertained to Harry Tomkins. Apparently no one connected to him had any claim on the property everyone thought had been his. His wife had really been the sole owner and had even had special papers drawn up at sometime during the short marriage to outline every financial transaction she had made to him. It seemed that Harry had spent a lot of his widow's money and didn't have anything to show for the exchanges.

Many people didn't know that Brunswick County was the largest county in North Carolina. It got its name from its first settlement, Brunswick Towne, on the banks of the Cape Fear River just below Wilmington. At that time, Brunswick County was not accessible to Wilmington by road; only by water. Few people outside of North Carolina natives realize that the very first colonial tea party was actually held in Brunswick Towne and not in Boston. At the time, the port of Wilmington was very important and so was the port at Brunswick Towne. The first act of rebellion against taxation without representation was held at the Brunswick Towne port at least 3 years prior to the Boston Tea Party that is remembered in our history books. Brunswick Towne is nothing but a colonial ruin these days although the NC

AUTHOR: DIANNE WARTH-VEREEN

Department of Archaeology and Preservation has done some excavations and does have a small museum on the premises. At one time, the governor of North Carolina had his residence at Brunswick Towne. The ruins of Russell borough are found here as well as those of the old St. Phillips Church whose walls still stand to emphasize that the colonists were God fearing people. Susie had photographs of all of the ruins because Kathryn had worked at the site while she had been in college. Kathryn had taken extensive photographs of all of the grounds and framed the ones Susie had liked the best. Many of Kathryn's photographs were used during Susie's genealogy presentations.

Susie likes to tell people during her lectures about the original people who lived on the land at Brunswick Towne, the Tuscarora Indians. Today there are signs along the road through what was once called the River Road that proclaims the land belongs to the Cape Fear Indian Trust. These have been nailed up by a gentleman who claims descent from the Cape Fear Indians who are a little known tribe that once inhabited the area. Orton Plantation is in this area. Orton was well known as a rice plantation and a turpentine plantation. Tar,

AUTHOR: DIANNE WARTH-VEREEN

pitch and turpentine were some of the stores that were shipped from Brunswick Towne in abundance. Maurice Moore is the person on record as founding Brunswick Towne in the year 1726. When Susie started to speak in her lectures, her face began to shine and her eyes would cloud over almost as if she were relaying her own memories to the audiences of people who came to learn the history of the area. There was no one else as well versed in the history of Brunswick County as Susie Carson. That was why she had received the designation of Brunswick County Official Historian.

Susie always enjoyed visiting Orton Plantation each spring to see the beauty of the gardens that were so well kept that they were one of the areas favorite tourist attractions. The Moore family built Orton in 1735, which makes it one of the oldest standing structures in Brunswick County. Recently she had begun to add the fact that the movie Fire Starter had been made there to her repertoire. The site was the venue for many weddings. It was a mark of social exception to have a wedding at the Orton chapel or even have one's wedding photos taken in the Orton gardens. These were all tidbits of information that Susie loved to include in her lectures about the history of Brunswick County. Recently, Orton had changed ownership. The plan was to return the plantation to a functioning rice plantation like it had been once long ago. That would be used in the lectures.

No doubt the court case involving the Gray family inheritance argument would find its way into the lectures, also. If it didn't find its way into the lectures, it would definitely find some space in Susie's weekly newspaper column. She had begun to write the chatty column several years before. She wrote interesting stories about the people that grew up in Southport and about its history. Often when she felt she needed either a break or a new perception, she would ask one of her many "children" to write their memories of a special time in their lives in Southport or some other part of Brunswick County.

Living in Brunswick County almost all of her life, Susie had become well known. First she was known as the legal secretary for Bunn Frink who was Brunswick County's very own Perry Mason. (I guess that made her Della Street).His cases were often high profile and were almost all criminal cases of some note. When Bunn closed his practice, Susie went back to work for E.J. Prevatte, (whom she had worked for in her early years as a legal secretary and private assistant) whose practice was devoted mostly to family practice and real estate law. In her years as the person at the desk through whom all knowledge eventually passed, Susie became so well known that people would often call to solicit her advice when they didn't think they had quite the need for a lawyer.

Working in high profile law offices had given Susie one of the sharpest minds in the county, if not the state. She loved to do crossword puzzles and often managed to do them in ink. She had a quick mind and was able to take small pieces of information and fit them together to make sense of them when even the smartest men in the profession were stumped. She sat at her desk with the Gray folder in front of her and wondered just what it was about Harry Tomkins' death that was tickling her brain so persistently.

"Jiggle," she spoke to the large brown woman who did the filing three times per week. "What do you remember about Harry Tomkins?"

"Mostly I remember that he was an ungrateful little brat when he was in school. He wouldn't sit still and he couldn't stay focused for more than five minutes at a time. He was mean to animals, too. I remember that." Hermoine Jigglesque had lived in Southport most of her life. She was on the shady side of seventy but she still had a lot of get-up-and-go left in her. She still managed to work three days a week and her time in the office was a big help to Susie. Jiggle had been a school teacher in Southport for only a few years before she had decided that she didn't like children enough to spend eight hours a day with someone else's. Harry Tomkins had been one of the deciding factors in her leaving the teaching profession. Her next profession was as a research librarian for the State Archives and History.

"Yes, he was mean to my own cats a few times. I never did understand how a child could be so mean at such a young age. It was almost like he was born with meanness just waiting to get out. I wonder if he ever calmed down."

"Well, from the number of wives he'd had, I doubt he got much nicer. Wouldn't a girl be satisfied with a good looking husband who had plenty of money if he were nice to her? I heard he could talk a good line but he wasn't much in the romance department, if you know what I mean." Susie blushed as she considered what

Jiggle was saying. "Funny though," she said"
that girl that was so crazy about him in high
school was here for the 4th. I wonder if they got
to see each other before he kicked off like that.
"

"Who are you talking about?" Susie's curiosity
was about to get the better of her.

"That Mills girl. What was she called? You
know the one whose mother owned that house
on the river where all the teachers had rooms.
She turned out to be a beautiful woman and
she can really sing those old songs."

"You mean Sparkie?" Susie remembered the
young girl who had grown into a willowy
blonde lounge singer. "Sparkie Mills and
Harry Tomkins? " The wheels in Susie's head
started to turn. Maybe she should call Minnie
and ask her if she knew about this supposed
high school romance. Maybe there was
something they needed to know about their
reunion.

AUTHOR: DIANNE WARTH-VEREEN

Six

"C.J., why didn't you tell me about Sparkie and Harry?" Minnie wondered why her friend had left out that little tidbit of knowledge. "Were they really an item? Did she see him while she was home? "

"I don't know. She mentioned that she might see him but she never said if she did or not. All I know is that she did a huge about face on the 4th and left without any explanation. There isn't anyone who can confirm that she was in the vicinity of the cars while they were being lined up for the parade. Nobody saw her around him. There were no records of any phone calls between them. Look, Minnie, you know I can't really talk about the case. Don't ask me anything else, ok?"

"Yeah; ok. Give me a call if you figure out anything. You know I will keep it to myself."

The two old friends said goodbye and both went back to their respective days.

Later on in the day, Oak Island Deputy Durbin noticed that a strange car was parked in front of the empty wooded lot next to Tomkins' house. He called in the license plate number and discovered it belonged to a man who lived in Calabash. The man didn't have a record and there were no warrants out for him so Deputy Durbin just noted the time and the make, model and color of the car and drove on to the west end of the island. He noticed that there were a lot of license tags from West Virginia and Ohio parked at the street ends and beach access areas. It was funny that so many people from those areas came to the beach each year. A lot of those summer visitors eventually retired and moved to the beach. They always said it was like a homecoming.

Harry Tomkins death had been a surprise. The man was fairly young; late fifties. He didn't seem to have any health problems. Maybe one of his ex-wives had finally gotten her revenge. Tomkins had been married several times and all the divorces had been quite acrimonious. Durbin pulled into the Blue Water Point parking lot and got out to check with the office manager and the guard regarding a call that had come in the previous night after all the 4th of July festivities were over. A guest in #6 had called 911 to report a woman had fallen (or maybe jumped) off of the end of the deep water dock around midnight. The dispatcher had sent an officer to answer the call and had contacted the Coast Guard at Oak Island so that they could send a boat to check it out. When he finally got to the dock he saw that the Coast Guard divers were still checking the area around the dock to see if they could find a body. The 911 caller claimed not to know who the person was. Of course, when the police deputy had arrived at Blue Water Point, they mysterious guest, who hadn't given his name, was gone. The office manager didn't have a record of a guest in #6. Since it was a local call, there was no record through the phone service.

"Chief Lee," called Deputy Durbin. "Have y'all found a body? Any clothes or anything?"

"No," responded the Coast Guard Chief. "We have had divers out here since sun up and we haven't found a thing. The tide turned about two hours ago and something should have floated by here by now if there was a jumper. Personally, I think that somebody was pulling your leg."

"Any idea why someone who wasn't registered in #6 would use the phone there to call 911 about a jumper who didn't exist?"

"No more than you have an idea how they got into #6 in the first place." Chief Lee was not amused. "I talked to Dolly in the office and she said that no one has come in at all since the 4th customers checked out. Have you guys checked out the cabin?"

"Yeah, Detective Chase and his partner made a quick sweep through there last night after the call came in. They didn't see anything."

"Think it might be a good idea to go through there more carefully before whatever evidence was there is gone?"

"I don't think Chase would be real happy if he heard I was second guessing him." Durbin had only been with the police department for a few weeks since he graduated from the local college course for criminal justice. Most of the police department was on-the-job trainees who had been there for several years. Durbin was not their favorite person. They called him the "College Professor" because he was always talking about something he had been taught in school.

"Maybe not but if you run up on something I bet the whole department would be a lot happier that they will be if they can't figure it out." Chief Lee stuck a cigarette in between his lips and held a match to it to light it.

AUTHOR: DIANNE WARTH-VEREEN

Durbin waved his hand in front of his face to keep the smoke from going up into his nose and eyes. He hated cigarette smoke even in the open air.

"Yeah, maybe I will check it out." He turned around and started back up the dock to land. In his mind he ran over the list of things to do when checking out a crime venue. He knew they had dusted for prints when they found out no one was registered in the room. He would just give the place a quick once over and get back on the road.

Durbin stopped by the office to pick up a key to #6 and carefully opened the door. The air conditioner had been left on about 73. It was cool inside. He made a mental note to turn the A/C off when he left the room. A quick glance around the 12 x 12 room told him that the person who had been there the previous night had been extremely neat and careful not to leave anything out of place. He noticed that the telephone book was open to a page with names beginning with T. He turned on the television and discovered it had been left on WECT, channel 6. Maybe whoever had called had been watching the 11:00 news. Cabin #6 was the only one that had a view of the deep water dock so it was possible that the

AUTHOR: DIANNE WARTH-VEREEN

inhabitant had actually seen someone. He
opened the door to the compact bathroom and
looked inside. All was neat and clean. It didn't
look like anyone had been inside at all. As he
was walking back into the main room he
noticed something pink on the floor and bent
down to see what it was. It was a fake finger
nail. There **had** been someone in the room last
night. He picked it up with his gloved hand
and dropped it into a tiny plastic evidence
tube and put it into his pocket. For whatever it
was worth, he had just found evidence that
someone had been in the room.

He walked back out to the parking lot and
noticed a person standing on one of the large
rocks at the edge of the water. It was difficult
to tell at a distance whether the person was a
man or a woman but the figure had sandy
blonde hair that was pulled back into a pony
tail and tied with a piece of string. He or she
wore poplin trousers rolled up to the top of the
calf and a white shirt with the sleeves rolled
up over the elbow. No shoes were in evidence.
As Durbin got nearer to the figure it turned
and walked away from him at a pace much
faster than the deputy could manage in his
heavy work shoes. As the land curved behind
some myrtle bushes, Durbin lost sight of the

AUTHOR: DIANNE WARTH-VEREEN

person. When he finally turned the corner the person was gone.

It was just another unexplained piece of information that had to be added to the case. Harry Tomkins had always been a pain in the tuchus and nothing had changed just because he was dead. Who had finally had enough of the self - loving weasel and gotten rid of him? Whoever it was deserved a medal and not an arrest warrant. He thought about the new Widow Tomkins; a former Miss North Carolina. How had Tomkins managed to snag her? She was beautiful and intelligent and had so much going for her. What did Harry Tomkins have to offer a woman like that? Durbin had heard through the grapevine that the widow had hired a private detective to delve into her husband's past only a few weeks prior to his death. He wondered what had prompted her to investigate something she had been so willing to overlook for the intervening years since they had met and gotten married. Had there been something in Tomkins past that he was desperate to hide and could it have led to his death? She sure was getting rid of any evidence that he had lived in that big house on Yacht Drive. He had seen the Habit for Humanity truck there three

AUTHOR: DIANNE WARTH-VEREEN

times in the past week loading up with stuff the Widow Tomkins was tossing out. Deputy Durbin made a mental note to check out Tomkins' family members who still lived in the area. His father still owned property there and his mother still lived over in Southport in an assisted living facility. He wondered why there hadn't been any announcement of service for the town's mayor. He was sure that Mayors who were still in office at the time of their death would be due a lot of pomp and circumstance. It seemed odd to have passed a week since his death with nothing but a short obituary in the State Port Pilot.

Durbin answered the shrill of his telephone and realized his caller was Sherriff Stone. "What can I do for you Sherriff?" he asked.

"Are you free? Could you meet me across the Swain's Cut Bridge at Worms and Coffee? I need to run something by you on the Tomkins case."

Durbin liked the lady sheriff who was currently in charge of law enforcement in Brunswick County. She was well liked but she didn't take any nonsense from anyone. Durbin had been delegated the "go to" guy for the Tomkins case by the Chief of Police of Oak

Island. At first he had thought it was an honor but he had come to think that might not be the case. No one seemed to want to get mixed up in whatever was going on.

He turned the car around and headed back toward Middleton and the "new" bridge. He expected the locals to call it that for a long time. They still dated things on the island "before and after Hazel" a terrible hurricane that had wiped the entire island clean in October of 1954. As he reached the stop light at the intersection of Middleton, NC 211 and Midway Road, he wondered what it was that the Chief wanted to talk to him about.

"Hey Durbin, thanks for meeting me here," said the Chief as she talked to him through the rolled down window of her patrol car. They had parked right beside the long part of the building; one facing the highway and one facing Worms and Coffee.

"No problem, Chief. What can I do for you? You said you had something you need to run by me?"

"Yes, it's sort of a touchy subject but Minnie Drew brought it to my attention and I thought we might have to start looking into it. Minnie

AUTHOR: DIANNE WARTH-VEREEN

and I went to high school together over in Southport, you know. She mentioned that there are a lot of people who disliked Harry Tomkins and some of them were people even I hadn't thought of. I know you have already gone over the long list of political opponents that he has aggravated during his years in local politics. He also had several friends in Raleigh that included a state senator who's been in office over 30 years, the former Secretary of State and several high placed members of the state departments of revenue and transportation. He went to school with a woman in the Department of Prisons. Here is her name and phone number. She just retired and moved to Greenville. She was something of a "party girl" in her day and I don't believe her current husband is aware of her past but she might know who would have it in for Tomkins. They remained close through the years. You need to keep it on the down low, of course. "She passed the typed information through the window of her car into the hands of Durbin who was seated in his car.

"I won't tell anyone how I got the name and number. I am sure there are a lot of people who knew the connection and could have remembered it if they had wanted to. The

Chief is getting antsy about all this. He seems kinda jumpy like he thinks the other shoe is about to drop or something."

"Yeah, with Harry you often had that feeling that the other shoe is about to drop. He always seemed to be right in the middle of some deal or other. He has done a lot of good for the area though. We don't need to forget that. He has been able to get us a lot of grants that we would never have been able to get if he hadn't known the right people to contact."

"What do you know about his family, Sherriff?"

"Just that his daddy was born here and still has a house over on the beach. I think he moved away when he and Harry's mother got divorced. He lives out west somewhere and comes back to the area for vacations. I understand that he and Harry's mother are both puzzled as to why the Widow Tomkins has been in such a hurry to divest her of anything that reminds her of their son. Why, Durbin? What are you thinking?"

"I am just wondering about the estate. You know, the widow is claiming that she owned everything and had from the start of the

AUTHOR: DIANNE WARTH-VEREEN

relationship. She claims that Harry was broke. He always acted like he was a millionaire without a care in the world. That car he drove was a special order and he had a small plane out there at the airport. There is supposed to be a yacht, too. How could he have all that and be broke? And if he owned any of it, who gets it? He'd been married, what, eight times? Did he have any kids with any of them or adopt any of their kids? "

"That's a pretty valid question and I'm not sure. I thought he had at least two children by different wives but I have not heard of them since their mothers divorced Harry so they could have been step children. I did hear that he had paid for several of his "significant others" to have abortions. Maybe one of them took the money and still had the child but I don't see how that could be a motive for murder."

"Sherriff, this is a strange case. It doesn't pass any smell test that I have ever heard of. Scuttlebutt is that Tomkins was seeing a woman over in Calabash about once a week. I have looked into her whereabouts on the 4th but she was in Caribou, Maine, at some sort of fishing lodge with her three brothers checking out a deal to buy a halibut fishing boat company. I heard she had asked Tomkins to help her raise funding to pay for the deal. She wouldn't have killed the golden goose, would she?"

"Like you say, Durbin, it's a weird case. Minnie said she would try to remember any other people Harry had been associated with over the years. Maybe there is someone from his past with a reason to want to kill him. You know, his wife hired a private detective about two weeks before his death. I haven't been able to get any information except that the agency is out of Phoenix, Arizona. The Wassum Agency, I think. They are famous for finding lost heirs for estates, adopted children, lost loves, tracking down old stocks and deeds and cold case type stuff. They solved that case last year where that woman and her 5 year old son walked out of their house one morning and were never heard of again. Turned out that the woman had information about a crime and the Marshall Service had taken her and the son in to protective custody and moved them into Witness Protection. It had been twenty years and they were still alive and living in some tiny little town on the Nevada/Utah border."

"I don't know why the Widow Tomkins would

want to hire someone like that. " The radio in the squad car blasted out a call and Durbin cranked the engine to leave. The Sherriff watched as he swiveled the car around and headed back across the "new" bridge. Something in the back of her mind kept bothering her but she just couldn't put her finger on what it was.

Seven

Sparkie Mills's feet hurt. She pulled the four inch stiletto heels off both feet and started to rub them briskly before sliding them into a pair of comfortable Birkenstocks that she had owned since college. She had finished her rehearsal and was ready to go home for a few hours rest before the show at midnight. At 40+ she was hardly the ideal choice for a midnight Vegas showgirl but she still did the occasional special show and this party for George Maloof fell in that category. She was grateful that her role in the show only involved sitting on the grand piano singing songs from the 30's and 40's. She had no objection to the beautiful designer evening gown that was on loan from one of the costume companies down on Sahara. The tag that was on it said it had come from the collection of Judy Garland's gowns. It had fit her perfectly; Judy had been petite and this had been from one of her "sizes" that still allowed for fitted gowns. The Palms was a great place to perform. This party was to be held in the penthouse auditorium that overlooked all the beautiful lights of Las Vegas. It was an honor to be asked to perform. She had enough time to have a long swim in the pool and lie out in the sun before her daughter got home from school and they had their "together" time.

She pointed the car toward the overpass and started around the beltway that would take her to the Green Valley area of Henderson. She was glad she didn't have to stop at Wal-Mart for anything because the parking lot was chock full as usual. She pulled over into the fast lane and pushed the pedal down to boost her past all of the cars that were heading back to their offices from long leisurely lunches. She saw the off ramp up ahead and pulled over into the right lane to get off. Not for the first time in the last few days, she noticed a green Toyota in her rear view mirror that seemed to be following her. She had seen it

AUTHOR: DIANNE WARTH-VEREEN

that morning when she had gone in to
rehearse and spotted it several days in a row
in the last week or so since she got back from
Southport. She mentally reviewed her budget
and her bills and decided that she hadn't let
anything slip that she should have paid.
Alexandra's tuition at the Toney private school
in Henderson was paid till the end of the year
so she didn't have to worry about that. Who
could be following her and why?

She pulled into her small driveway and
parked her car in the garage that was
attached to her yellow bungalow. The house
had been built in the 1940's when Vegas was
just starting to grow. The original owners had
been retired bit players from MGM and had
moved to Vegas because the climate was much
the same as that in California and no one
seemed to be surprised to see a movie star in
the frozen food section of the supermarket.
They had kept the little house in pristine
condition until the death of the woman. The
man couldn't bring himself to stay there
without his wife and put it up for sale just
before Sparkie came to Vegas. She hadn't had
the money to buy the place but in the end she
had met the owner and worked out a deal.
She became his boarder. As he aged, she saw

AUTHOR: DIANNE WARTH-VEREEN

that his clothes were clean and his meals were cooked and took care of his house. In return, he left her the house in his will. She had legally changed her last name to his and anyone who had known the old man thought Sparkie and Alexandra were his close relatives.

Sparkie had never told anyone at home about Alexandra. They also didn't know she had changed her last name. She Was Sparkie Mills in Southport and at work but here on Warbler Lane she Was Sandra Wilson who lived here with her daughter Alexandra and their nanny, Theresa. The little bungalow was her safe haven. Here she didn't have to remember the bad times. She didn't have to think about leaving home and never looking back. Here she was who she wanted to be and she wasn't a disappointment to anyone.

She shucked off her rehearsal clothes and pulled on her black one piece swim suit. Grabbing a soda from the fridge she pushed the glass door aside and went out to the pool. She took a gulp of the soda and then immersed herself in the refreshing water. She turned over on her back and floated for a while, unaware that the green Toyota had stopped in front of her house and that the occupant was

AUTHOR: DIANNE WARTH-VEREEN

taking photographs with a telephoto lens.

Theresa called to her when it was nearly time for Alexandra to come in from school. It was someone else's day to pick the kids up from school. Three mothers took turns going out to the lake to the private enclave that guarded their precious children from 8 in the morning until 3 in the afternoon, five days a week. She reluctantly pulled herself out of the water and toweled off with one of the big fluffy towels from the Hilton Hotel where she had worked for several months the previous winter. She had a few minutes to shower and get dressed before Alexandra would be home calling for pizza or tacos. She smiled as she thought about her daughter. It had not been the easiest thing in the world to raise a daughter all on her own in Las Vegas, Nevada. She would have much rather have afforded her the type of life that growing up in Southport would have given her but it hadn't been possible. She had resigned herself to living without family or friends while her daughter grew up as far away from her hometown as possible. Girls just didn't raise children on their own in Southport. Anyone who chose to do so found themselves the subject of gossip and snide remarks and soon moved away or

AUTHOR: DIANNE WARTH-VEREEN

fell into another mismatched marriage just to be "one of a couple."

It had been years before she had contacted anyone in her hometown once she had left. She had known that she had to cut the cord for good and never would have reconnected with CJ if she hadn't needed to know about her family. Once she and CJ had started talking again it was as if they had never stopped communicating.

God, she wished she had never let CJ talk her into going back to Southport for the 4th of July.

Eight

Nancy Sanders had worked for Brunswick County in their forensics lab for quite a while. Her father, Quack Sanders, owned Quack's Sea Shack in the old Yacht Basin section of Southport and was one of the best chefs in the state. He was famous for his local seafood and "sides". Nancy had trained as a paramedic and worked the local rescue squads until she had finished her forensics courses. The lab she ran had been put together with a grant that everyone said would never come through but Harry Tomkins had managed to convince the

people with the money that even a little place
like Brunswick County needed a good
forensics lab to solve those murders and cases
that were lying in the cold case files. That had
been two years ago and Nancy had been in her
element ever since.

Nancy had been on duty in the lab when the
call had come in about Harry Tomkins. She
and Harry had gone to school together
beginning in the first grade. It had been quite
a shock to see him lying on that gurney stiff
and dead on the 4th of July. The County
Coroner had not had any idea what had
happened. She had been baffled, too. The
autopsy performed in Chapel Hill hadn't found
anything to indicate that there had been foul
play but it also hadn't found anything to
indicate that he had croaked of natural causes,
either. She was the last bastion of hope to find
out what had happened. Usually she loved
trying to solve the unsolvable but this time
she just felt stressed beyond belief.

She studied the autopsy report once more in
hopes of being able to figure out what had
happened. CJ had asked her if she would
study the report again to see if there was
anything that might have been missed. So far,
Nancy had not found anything odd. Well,

AUTHOR: DIANNE WARTH-VEREEN

except maybe the state of Harry's bronchial tubes. They had been awfully inflamed. She had checked with his doctor and Harry had been diagnosed with chronic bronchitis and emphysema. That hadn't really been much of a surprise because Harry had been a three pack a day smoker. She doubted that he had cut down much once he had discovered he had emphysema, either. Harry was one of those people who considered it **his** business if he died of lung cancer from smoking or not.

She smiled as she thought of the evenings at the Back Street Café in the little alley that led to the yacht basin where she and Kyra and Harry had all hung out together. They had gathered every evening after work for supper and friendship. None of them had been married at the time; "in between" as Kyra used to say. She remembered how well the two of them had danced together. They had won every Shag contest that they had entered. The easy shuffling steps to the beach, boogie and blues music always brought back memories of Kyra who had passed away way too young. There would never be another person like her. If Harry had found his way to Heaven then Kyra had surely been there to let him in.

AUTHOR: DIANNE WARTH-VEREEN

Nancy read the autopsy report for the third time and then turned her attention to the pile of medical records that Mr. Tomkins had been kind enough to let her look at. Harry's father didn't think his son had died of natural causes but he didn't think anyone hated him enough to murder him either. He had released the medical records to Nancy so she could check and see if there was anything that could have triggered a sudden death.

The clock struck two and she realized that she only had one more hour until the end of the day. She picked up the phone to call CJ and to tell her that the medical records had finally arrived from Harry's father. It didn't look much like the fancy equipment in the lab was going to do this case even one bit of good.

"Hey, CJ, I got the records this morning. I haven't been able to find any reason so far why he should have just up and died from sitting in a car waiting for the parade to start. Yeah, I know that he and what's-his-name hated each other but I don't think that kind of hate can kill you that fast. There is something else here that we are all missing. I know it's here. I just have to keep looking until I find it. Did you talk to Durbin yet? Any word on what's happening over at the beach these

AUTHOR: DIANNE WARTH-VEREEN

days? "

"No. Something weird down at the point but nothing came of it and I don't think it had anything to do with Harry's case anyway. Do you think Mr. Tomkins knows anything that could help us?"

"No. If he did he would tell us. He is just sick about all this. Harry's mother, on the other hand, couldn't be bothered to even talk to me about her newly deceased son. She was too busy playing bridge and having lunch with her friends."

"Let me know the minute you come up with something."

"Yeah! I'm a regular Abby like from that program NCIS. "She laughed as she hung up the phone.

Nine

"That was the most amazing party!"

"WOW!"

AUTHOR: DIANNE WARTH-VEREEN

THE SUSIE CARSON HISTORY

MYSTERIES

"How much do you think this party cost?"

"These were just some of the comments heard last night after the midnight surprise party given at the Palms Resort and Casino for George Maloof. "The television reporter was smiling as she showed off the colorful photographs from the previous night's entertainment gala. "No expense was spared by the billionaire's family in planning this party to honor the Las Vegas Man of the Year. Sparkie Mills, local chanteuse, sang a medley of Cole Porter songs as well as selections from Broadway shows of the 30's and 40's. She was accompanied by well-known pianist and singer Harry Connick, Jr. who also joined her in several duets. Ms. Mills wore a gown from the collection of the famous mother of Liza Minnelli, Judy Garland. Liza was also on hand to do many of her mother's songs as well as some of her own. Her friendship with the Maloof family is well known in the Las Vegas area and no one was surprised when just after midnight a huge cake was rolled into the room and out jumped the curvy gamine Minelli dressed in black fishnet stockings and a romper suit style tuxedo. Maloof's Man of the Year award was clutched in her hands and she presented it to him with her usual aplomb.

AUTHOR: DIANNE WARTH-VEREEN

Instead of the usual boring speeches about how much the award winner had contributed to the city, the Mayor just thanked Maloof and his family for helping to raise the "tone" in the local casinos back to the elegance of the earlier days. No one can say just how much the celebration set the Maloof family back but it is reported that only the best champagne and caviar were served. The party lasted until the early hours this morning. Paris Hilton, George Clooney, Russell Crowe, Julia Roberts, and Sean, Puffy, Combs were on the guest list and among the last to leave the revolving party room at the top of the Palms resort."

Photos accompanied the report as did a short video. Once the report was finished and the air time given back to the studio, the mood switched back to seriousness, health care, the environment and the economy. The tall man who was seated at the end of the bar in the lounge of Caesar's Palace had watched with interest as the video of the entertainment for the previous evening had been shown. Sparkie Millis looked like she was the epitome of a famous singer making a cameo appearance for a friend. Even Liza "with a Z" didn't compare to her for glamour. She had a lovely voice and the songs that she sang had been perfectly

married to it. The sound was that of the 30'
and 40's when famous band leaders like Benny
Goodman had showcased their music with
beautiful blonde or brunette singers standing
in the spotlight. He wondered how she had
managed to get a dress once owned by Judy
Garland and how her daughter really felt
about sharing the spotlight with her mother
again (even if it was just her dress).

He motioned to the bartender for another shot
of Scotch and fumbled in his shirt pocket for
his cigarettes. It was a nasty habit and he had
often sworn to kick it but he had never
managed to do it. He pulled his cell phone out
of his coat pocket and typed in a text message.
It took only a few seconds to get a response. It
was short and to the point. "Continue as
directed." Well, there wasn't anything else to
do then. He might as well go ahead and make
his plane reservations or he would never be
able to get out of McCarran before the
weekend arrived. Geez it was hot. Vegas could
easily sport a temperature of 112 degrees in
July and he thought it had reached it that day.
Even the first class air conditioning of
Caesar's didn't seem to be cutting the thick
heat. He gulped his shot of Scotch and slapped
a fifty dollar bill down on the bar for the

AUTHOR: DIANNE WARTH-VEREEN

bartender to settle his bill and leave a generous tip. He could afford it. This gig was paying well and it looked like it would be going on for awhile.

He stood and started toward the door of the lounge. His eye caught the movement of a tall willowy blonde as she scooted towards the stage area at the back of the room. Sparkie Mills had arrived for her rehearsal for tonight's show. He decided to stick around and see if he could manage to "run into her" before he headed for the hotel to pack and make his reservations. He knew from the people he had interviewed that she rarely dated and when she did it was one of three people she had known for years. No one would divulge where she lived but he had followed her to a small yellow bungalow in Green Valley. He had taken photos with the high powered telephoto lens that was attached to his new digital camera. He loved that camera. It would hold several thousand photos on one little digital disc that he could remove if he had to take photos of another case. Modern inventions were wonderful.

He had managed to get close enough to the stage to hear what was going on when Sparkie's cell phone rang.

AUTHOR: DIANNE WARTH-VEREEN

"What? Are you sure it's broken? Which hospital did they take her to? St. Rose? Okay, I'll go there immediately. Tell the Sister that's with her that she has her insurance information in her personal information at school if they need to access it before I get there. I am over on the Strip so it will take me about thirty minutes at least to get there. No, Theresa is visiting her mother today so she can't go. It's no problem. My daughter always comes first with me." As she hung up he noticed the pain in her eyes and her worried expression as she talked to the producer and the music director before she grabbed her purse to leave.

A daughter; he hadn't known anything about a daughter. Neither had anyone he had interviewed for information on her. Miss Sparkie Mills had a secret life. That was certainly very interesting. He pulled his cell phone out of his pocket and sent another text message.

AUTHOR: DIANNE WARTH-VEREEN

Ten

"I just don't believe that the Mills girl had anything to do with Harry Tomkins' death." said Susie as she ate her lunch. Her companion at the lunch counter of Green's Drug and Variety Store on Front Street in Wilmington was Annie Mae Woodside, one of her closest friends. They often came to Wilmington to shop and spend a relaxing day visiting places and people who were special to them both. This day they had come to visit Mary Mintz, nee' Cranmer, once a local Southport woman, who was married to Judge Rudolph Mintz. Susie wanted her advice on music for a special evening being planned for the Historical Society anniversary celebration to be held in September. Mary was an excellent pianist and music was something she knew a great deal about. The theme was to be the early days when Southport was still known as Smithville. Suzie planned to use a replica of the gate that used to be at the edge of the town as part of the decorations in the Community Building. Many of the locals had said it would be better if the gate still stood.

AUTHOR: DIANNE WARTH-VEREEN

Southport had been one of the first "gated communities." Bette Leggett was hand lettering some signs and Water's Thompson was painting a mural on several huge pieces of paper that were to be hung on one of the large blank walls. He intended to display many of the old homes and buildings that no longer existed including the huge Cranmer house that once stood next to the Indian Trail Tree where the library stood now.

"I don't either, Susie. She was always a lovely girl. I remember her from her younger days when she used to come by my house and sit on the porch and pet my old Persian cat, Sheila. She was very intelligent and starved for knowledge. She read all the books I loaned her and always asked if there were any more. She used to sing to my cat and she had a wonderful voice even then. I think she did go out with Harry for a little while but I don't know if it was serious. I know she wouldn't have done anything bad even if she'd had the chance. There are just some people who you know are good and Sparkie was one of them. I never understood why she left Southport like she did or why she never came back until this year."

"Minnie Drew keeps saying that there is

AUTHOR: DIANNE WARTH-VEREEN

something really strange about this whole case. Of course, she always sees a mystery in everything that doesn't have a patent explanation. She and Kathryn have been friends since they were babies. Her mother and my sister, Thelma, were good friends in school. She is like a member of my family. I always carefully consider anything she says; even if it is just based on a "feeling".

"Well, that's about all any of us have to go on, isn't it?" Miss Annie Mae said between bites of toasted chicken salad sandwich. "CJ Stone doesn't seem to have any answers either. I saw her in Watson's yesterday and she said Harry's widow has sold his car, has the house up for sale and has given away most of his personal possessions. It doesn't sound like she is grieving very much, does it? Of course, she wasn't anywhere around when Harry died so she can't be a suspect if it is determined that he died by foul play."

"That is true. I guess she could have hired someone though," said Susie. She picked up a French fry with her fork and dipped it in a little pool of catsup that she had poured on her plate.

"Well, there still isn't anything to indicate that

AUTHOR: DIANNE WARTH-VEREEN

someone killed him. He was an aggravating little boy. He was always so sure of himself. His father worked hard to put food on their table and his mother spent it as fast as he made it. If they hadn't lived with his mother on the beach they probably couldn't have maintained a home. Harry always seemed like he thought he was "entitled" to expect the best of everything and as he grew up he continued with that manner of thinking. He's managed to attract women by buying them fur coats and diamonds but the money was never his own; it was his father's. It probably is true that his widow owned all of the personal and real property. Still, that's a reason for **him** to kill **her**, not vice versa."

"Have you been reading Agatha Christie again, Annie Mae?" Susie thought that her friend secretly longed to be like the adventurous mystery writer whose books never seemed to go out of popularity.

"I think I should point out that it was I who discovered that the old church secretary had been taking twenty dollars a week out of the weekly collection money."

"True, you did. You also figured out that the county auditor wasn't really keeping track of all the money collected for dog tags, either."

They laughed as they finished their lunch and then walked next door to Effird's Department Store where they shopped for new hats and gloves. Wilmington had two large department stores at which to buy women's clothing. Effird's was the smaller and older of the two. Belk's was the larger and newer and shopping there was a passport to all the newest clothing labels that were being sold in the South. Susie's weakness was shoes. Kathryn could copy almost any article of clothing and make it look like it had come straight off the rack at the department store so all Susie had to do was buy the accessories that made her look like she had just stepped off a fashion show runway.

Annie Mae also liked to dress well but she usually bought her clothing at one of the more exclusive clothing stores on Front Street that catered to the business woman's styles and needs. She was the first female to be hired as County School Superintendent and she did her best to keep up her image. They finished their lunch and took a walk to Gurr's Jewelry. Mrs. Gurr was excited to share the newest shipment of pearl jewelry with them.

AUTHOR: DIANNE WARTH-VEREEN

 Next stop was McClelland's and then Woolworth's. The day's adventure's ended with milkshakes at Tom's Drug Store soda fountain on the corner of Market and Front St. They continuously talked about the Tomkins case and whether or not Harry had been murdered. It was very confusing because although many people disliked him no one seemed to have a genuine reason to kill him.

Eleven

Alexandra came out the emergency room cubby with her left arm in a sling and her left foot in a navy blue boot to protect it from further damage. Sparkie exited right behind her talking to a tall Hispanic doctor in a white lab coat. It was obvious that they were friends from the arm the doctor had around her shoulders. He would have to find out how long the doctor had been at the hospital and how long he and Sparkie had been friends. His boss had said he should find out who the girl's father might be but he didn't know exactly where to start. Obviously the girl hadn't been born in Southport because no one knew about

AUTHOR: DIANNE WARTH-VEREEN

her existence. He texted his employer about the girl's injury and followed the couple as they exited hospital.

The car pulled out onto Boulder Highway and drove east. He followed it until it turned into the parking lot at the Railroad Pass Casino. The sign out front read "Prime Rib dinner $5.99 until 4PM" and he knew that they were going for a "comfort meal". He decided to go inside and get a sandwich and watch them for awhile. No one knew what he looked like so they wouldn't spot him.

They were sitting in a booth at the back of the coffee shop. The doctor wasn't with them; it was just the two females. He took a table for one nearby and listened to their conversation but he didn't learn anything important that he could report to his employer. Sparkie Mills was a complicated bit of business. He couldn't figure out just how she had anything to do with his employer. His hearing focused on them when he heard Sparkie mention that she had talked to Sheriff Stone just that very morning.

"She wants me to come back to Southport for a few days, darlin' and I think I might. I didn't get a chance to see everyone I wanted durin' the Fourth." Sparkie put a forkful of baked potato in her mouth and watched to see what her daughter would say.

"Mom, why haven't you ever taken me to Southport? I would like to see where you grew up and where my family roots began." Her daughter had a soft voice with a lilt of music in it.

"Oh, honey, I didn't have too many happy days in Southport. There aren't any family members left for you to meet and no one who remembers my parents that could tell you anything about them. I opened a few old doors when I was there and I just would like a chance to make certain I closed them tight again. Believe me, Alexandra, there isn't anything in Southport for you and me."

Alexandra decided, as teenagers usually do, that there really was something in Southport. She wanted to know what it was that her mother was hiding from her. She never talked much about her time there and only briefly mentioned any of her old friends. She knew that her mother often saw CJ Stone and that she was the person who had talked Sparkie into going back to Southport to honor Mrs. Carson, someone who had been a mentor to her mother as a girl.

She finished her dinner and milkshake wondering why her mother was always so sad. Often she would see her staring off into space as if she was in another world or find her, book turned face down in her lap, with tears in her eyes and starting to spill out onto her cheeks. Whenever she tried to ask her about it, her mother would say "I will explain it all someday when you are old enough to understand." Well, at seventeen, she thought she was old enough to understand just about anything her mother could tell her. She decided to ask Theresa what she knew about her mother's past. She had been employed by Sparkie when Alexandra was just a baby and was now more like a permanent fixture in their lives. Theresa would tell her if she knew anything. It was time.

On the ride back to Green Valley they didn't talk about Southport or the past. They discussed how Alexandra had been injured and how her recovery would affect the remainder of the school year. She enjoyed the many sports she played for the school and had been looking forward to the upcoming tennis season. She knew she would be sidelined for several weeks if she did not follow the doctor's instructions to the letter.

"Mom, I think I might sign up for one of the online courses from UNLV for the spring semester since I won't be playing tennis for the first of the season."

"That's a good idea, Sweetie. It might give you a leg up on some of the courses for your freshman year. What were you thinking about taking?"

"I was thinking about taking freshman math before I forget everything I ever learned. Dulce Sessions said that she nearly forgot everything after the first semester at college because she had so much new stuff crowding it out. "

"Getting the math out of the way is good idea but I don't think you'll forget what you have already learned. Take the harder courses online and in summer school once you actually start college and you will be able to concentrate more."

"I'm glad we're on the same page, Mom. So many of the people I know have gotten burnt out early in college."

"They aren't burnt out because of studying, Alex. In some cases, there is a lot of hard partying going on. I don't think a lot of the kids realize how difficult life will be in the real world. In fact, most of them have never seen the real world."

"I know, Mom." Alexandra sighed. She knew her mother had put her whole life aside just for her. She never seemed to have a personal life and she worked all hours at her job at the casino and doing special party entertainment. She had to respect her mother's work ethic. She never just stayed home because she didn't "feel well". There were many times when Alex knew her mother needed a break but she never took one. She was determined to not have a life like that.

"Oh, look, that new store is open. Let's check it out." Sparkie turned into the small strip shopping center that was near the beginning of their housing area. The store, Doll Clothes, was an enigma. There had been paper on all of the show windows since the name had been posted. No one had any idea what the stock was going to be and Sparkie and Alexandria were eager to see what was being offered.

They walked through the heavily carved door that was at the entry to the store. Inside, the walls were covered with mirror board creating

AUTHOR: DIANNE WARTH-VEREEN

the illusion that the stock was endless as were the shelves and peg board items. What caught both women's eye first was the shoe display that offered many designer name brands. Alexandra still preferred Papagallos but Sparkie's eye landed on a pair of stiletto heels with wisps of feathers attached to the thin, tiny straps and clear Lucite heels with tiny little birds inside.

It was a store filled with the most unique accessories that Sparkie had ever seen. Alexandra was engrossed by the latest clothes seen on her favorite models, singers or actresses. They had never seen anything like it. It was amazing. Sparkie made her way to speak to the woman behind the check out counter. She asked her what the owners of the store based their buying policies on.

"Actually, there are three owners." answered the woman in a voice that had an English accent. "I am the main owner. My name is Emilee Chatsworth and I am from London. My partners are Justin Foushee who is based in New York but also has offices in Paris and Milan where the best fashion houses are and my final partner is Giselle Ayars who has worked as a buyer for great department stores such as Neiman Marcus, Bonwit Teller, Bon

Marche, and others from Europe and South
America. We choose our items because they
catch our eye, so to speak. We sell one of a
kind items. There will be brands you are
familiar with as well as designers you have
never heard of but you will not find more than
one item of a kind. The young lady with you is
certainly a beauty. Is she your daughter?"

"Yes, she is my daughter Alexandra. I am
Sandra Wilson. My friends call me Sparkie."
She extended her hand to the English woman
with a smile that told her she agreed with her
policies 100%.

"Do you think your daughter would be
interested in doing some ad modeling for our
little shop? She has the look we are looking for
even in her school uniform and her injury
wrappings. "She smiled at Sparkie. "Your
daughter has beautiful skin that is not caked
with gobs of makeup. Her eyes would rival
those of Elizabeth Taylor and she isn't even
wearing heavy layers of mascara or shadow.
You do not find natural beauty like that just
walking into your to look at your inventory."

"Alexa," Sparkie called to her daughter who
had found her way to the section of the store
that displayed items and styles imported from

Paris and Milan just a few weeks before. Alexandra turned and walked to the front of the store where her mother was talking to the owner. "This is Emilee Chatsworth, one of the owners of the store. She was wondering if you would like to do a little modeling for her."

"Oh, wow, would I? Are you serious?"

"Yes, if your mother approves. You are slim enough to show off the clothing to advantage without being bone thin. You already have beautiful skin and hair and I think you will photograph beautifully. My partners and I were getting ready to comb the modeling databases but I believe an unknown local beauty will be much more interesting. We have several of these stores that we have recently opened worldwide and I think you will be a strong model and representative. Of course, we will schedule everything around your school schedule until spring break and summer vacation. If you are interested we can do some test photographs on Saturday."

"Can I, Mom?"

"Let me consider it tonight and I will talk to Ms. Chatsworth again tomorrow."

"Great!"

AUTHOR: DIANNE WARTH-VEREEN

Twelve

The print ads turned out well and Alexandra got her first paycheck about a week after the first time they walked into the new boutique. Sparkie felt that it wasn't anything to worry about but she had never let Alexandra be photographed for any publications that might be seen outside of Vegas before. She had many reasons to be careful but none that she wanted to have to discuss with Alex. Ever since Alex had been an infant she had been beautiful. She did not have the teen aged skin of her friends peppered with blemishes. Alex's skin was smooth and remained untouched by make up except for a little lip gloss that Sparkie had agreed for her to wear now that she was in high school. She wore her hair long and straight. Often she sported pigtails or a pony tail but she never curled her hair. She enjoyed doing the print ads for the store but she didn't aspire to being a model. She had seen what happened to high school girls and guys who got caught up in that life and the life of performing on the stage. To Alex it was just a plot for a sitcom or movie. She intended to do something important with her life. To Alex, grades were everything. She wanted to make Sparkie proud of her and maybe one day is able to provide for Sparkie like she had done for her all of her young life. She didn't even mind that she attended a year 'round school.

The man with the camera kept riding by school and by their house and snapping photos of Alex to provide for his boss. No one really noticed another car along the roads of Green Valley. The freeway was close enough that people often took short cuts through the residential areas to get to the south end of strip. Alex was never alone long enough for him to take a chance and speak to her.

In North Carolina, the case of Harry Tompkins had reached a stand still. His widow had successfully off- loaded his car and boat and even had a contract on the house they had shared. No one even bothered to speculate who had killed him any more. It had become a moot point because there didn't seem to be any answer. C.J. had called Sparkie several times and still hadn't found out if she had actually seen or talked to Harry while she was in

Southport for the 4th of July. There was something about the whole case that baffled everyone who bothered to think about it. The body had finally been released to his parents and then cremated. The parents had held a small and tasteful memorial service that concentrated on his years of public service to the area. Instead of flowers, the parents had asked for donations to a fund to help create a scholarship for a deserving local high school senior to a state college for a major in political science. It made the front page of the local paper but was only given a couple of columns. It was sad that a man's life could be reduced to some print in a paper.

C.J. called Sparkie and suggested they get together for a girl's weekend but Sparkie couldn't take time off from work since she was headlining in a remake of the Broadway show Promise Her Anything. The big stage at the newest mega resort on the Strip was taking the town of Las Vegas by storm. Sparkie had reluctantly given up her job in the lounge at Caesar's Palace to take the role of understudy to the lead just a few days after Alex's accident. She was hoping it would lead to a better part at a later date but she didn't have to wait as long as she expected to. Flitzy Paris slipped while walking through the casino two hours after a show one night. She broke her leg and hip when she got tangled up in the Wheel of Fortune display of slot machines on the mezzanine near the front door. Sparkie became the headliner overnight and had been on an upward course ever since.

Because she wanted her old hometown friend to see how well she was doing, Sparkie went against her own better judgment and invited C.J. out to see the show. Since Alex hadn't ever seen the show and had been asking about Southport, she went against her judgment a second time and had Alex attend the show with C.J. After the show was over they went backstage to see Sparkie. The dressing room was filled with flowers and cards and congratulations.

"Sparkie, I can't believe you never told me you have a daughter." C.J. mentally calculated the year Alex had been born from the age she had been given. Was there some connection between Alex's parentage and when Sparkie left Southport? She asked herself how to broach this question with Sparkie?

"Yeah, well, Alex is pretty special to me, C.J. and I pretty much keep her and Southport separate."

"That's true, Ms. C.J." Alex smiled at her and then continued her sentence. "I have asked about Southport and her family but I always get the same answer; 'someday I will tell you all about it'."

"Come on, C.J." said Sparkie to her friend. "Let's drop Alex off at home and go get something to eat; I'm starving." They were in the parking lot getting into Sparkie's car. The sky was clear except for the thousands of sparkling stars that dotted it like diamonds. "Go on to bed. C.J. and I are going to the casino's midnight buffet and then spend some time talking before I come back home. "

"Will I see you again, Ms. C.J.?"

"Well, not this trip but I am sure we will see each other again. It was great meeting you, Alex. You are certainly a smart and pretty young lady. Your mother tells me you have even done some modeling for one of the local boutiques."

"Yes, I have. It was a lot of fun but I wouldn't want to be a model full time. The kids at

AUTHOR: DIANNE WARTH-VEREEN

school all liked the magazine ads they saw. I was famous for about five minutes but, then, that's about how long fame usually lasts. "

As they turned into the boulevard at the entry of Green Valley Ranches, C.J. leaned back in the passenger seat and closed her eyes. She needed to think. Was it possible that Alex was Harry Tompkins' daughter? Could that be why Sparkie never came back to Southport? Even more important, could that be why Harry Tompkins was now just an urn filled with ashes sitting on his Mother's bedside table? She opened her eyes long enough to see the small lane where Sparkie lived and admire the little cottage that had been her home with Alex for the past fifteen or so years. It was a very nice little house and the yard was well landscaped, too. How had Sparkie been able to afford that on her salary as a waitress or even as a lounge singer? Something here didn't quite add up. Maybe she should have a talk with Sparkie and see what she could find out.

Alex got out of the car in the driveway and Sparkie remained parked there until she was safely inside and had called on her cell phone to tell her mother that everything was fine. Sparkie flung her right arm over the back of the car seat and started to back out of the driveway but had to stop long enough for a dark sedan to drive past the house.

"I know I have seen that car already at least once today," she said to C.J.

"Why is that odd, Sparkie? It's a road and cars drive on roads all the time."

"Yes, but this is a dead end road and mine is the last house before that big estate that Jerry Lewis used to own. There is no way that car came from that estate. The only people that ever go there drive cars worth way more than that P.O.S." Sparkie laughed at her own joke.

"Where are we going now, Sparkie? I'm not used to eating a big meal this late at night."

"Where Las Vegas is concerned, time doesn't matter, "Sparkie smiled and replied. "I thought I would give you The Tour, girlfriend."

"The Tour?" asked C.J. questioningly.

"Yeah. The times you have been out here I don't think I have ever taken the   time to show you around the Strip. You know, you can go from modern day New York City to a castle in the days of the Knights of Merry Olde England. Then you can go to Paris and Venice

just by getting on the tram. If you're bored, we
can check out the circus. If you want Chinese
there are two casinos that will give you the
best choices you can have. You can even visit
the pyramids and the treasures of King Tut.
You never have to even leave the Strip.
Sometimes it's an overload on tourists. There
are buffets that a king would kill for and if you
have the money, you can party with the
richest people on earth. It's an adult's Disney
World. Sometimes I forget who I am and why I
am here. It's wonderful, C.J. I don't have to
think about living in Southport and knowing I
wasn't smart enough to get a scholarship to a
college. I don't have to remember that my
mama made all my clothes and that my shoes
came from the Pic and Pay over on Carolina
Beach Road. I can pretend I bought my shoes
at Su Anne and my clothes at the Wonder
Shop or Justin's. No one knows me here, C.J.
and I like that. I haven't made a lot of friends
on purpose. I don't want Alex to ever know
what life was like when I was a kid her age. I
want her to think I was the most popular girl
in school and that I went steady with the boy
of my dreams. I want her to think I left home
and came out here because I was so talented
that a scout found me and gave me the
backing and attention that I needed to make it

AUTHOR: DIANNE WARTH-VEREEN

big. I don't want her to ever have to struggle or worry about whether she will feed her child or pay the light bill. That's why I never told you about Alex, C.J. I have to keep her and Southport away from each other in my life and my mind. Most of all, I have to keep her away from Southport in my heart."

"Who's Alex's father, Sparkie?"

"You know I'm not going to tell you that, C.J."

"Was it Harry Tompkins?" The car turned into the parking lot at the Mandalay Bay. They left it with the valet and C.J. followed Sparkie in through the casino's rotating doors and up the stairs to the midnight buffet. She smiled at the girl at the check out stand and paid for two meals. Indicating to C.J. that she should help herself to any of the areas of food and meet her in the banquet seating in the corner near the big aquarium. Sparkie went over and made a big salad in the large bowl and then she sat down and wiggled her fingers in the air to indicate to the cocktail waitress that she was ready to order drinks. She ordered each of them a flute of champagne. Might as well get ready for C.J.'s questions.

AUTHOR: DIANNE WARTH-VEREEN

Thirteen

"I don't think there is another test to be run, C.J." said Nancy as she talked to her friend in her capacity of forensics expert to county sheriff. "I have run everything I can think of. There has to be something we don't know. What did you find out from your trip out to see Sparkie?"

Nancy had graduated a year or so behind C.J. and was about that much older than Sparkie Mills. She had been aware of the big crush that Sparkie had on Harry when she was in high school and he was in college. She didn't believe that Sparkie had any bearing on the death but she had to cover all the bases.

"Sparkie wasn't very forthcoming, Nancy. She told me a few things I didn't know but mostly she just refused to talk about why she left Southport all those years ago and she definitely wouldn't talk about the 4th of July. She's hiding something big; I'm sure of it. I'm just not sure what it is that she's hiding. "She sighed and Nancy could hear the frustration in her friend's voice.

AUTHOR: DIANNE WARTH-VEREEN

"Sparkie has a   daughter, Nancy. Did you know that?"

"What? No, I don't believe it."

"Well, you better because I met her. She doesn't really look a lot like Sparkie; must take after her father. Wonder who he was?"

"She didn't tell you?"

"No. She clamed right up. Said she kept Alex separate from her life in Southport."

"You don't think……?"

"To be honest, I don't have any idea what to think. I didn't know Sparkie very well   when I was in school. I don't remember her having any attachment to anyone; much less Harry. Oh, come on! You don't think that's why she left here? How old is the girl? "

"I don't know, exactly. It was sort of awkward and I was only alone with her while we were at the show and Sparkie was on stage. I couldn't talk to her then. She never mentioned her dad and Sparkie didn't tell me a thing when we were alone later. She made it clear she wasn't going to talk about it. She did ask if anyone had ever come up with anything

AUTHOR: DIANNE WARTH-VEREEN

in Harry's death, though."

"The only thing that stands out after another autopsy is some hairs found in the lungs. They were so tiny that it hasn't been easy coming up with an identity. I am still working on that. C.J., that's the only new thing I have found. You made a bigger splash telling me that Sparkie has a teenaged daughter.

The telephone in the lab rang and Nancy reached over to answer it. "Oh, hello, Miss Susie. Yes, C.J. is here and we were just talking about Harry's case. No, I don't think I have anything new to tell you. I am checking on something that *may* mean something but I doubt it. I think we are stymied."

She smiled as she talked to her friend and mentor and then she said, "Dudley is missing again? Doesn't that cat ever stay where he is supposed to? No, don't worry; I will be on the lookout for him here at the courthouse. He often makes his way into Miss Vickie's office to see if she saved him anything from lunch. If he shows up I'll bring him home. Talk to you later."

C.J. smiled at Nancy and shook her head. "Remember how Miss Susie figured out who

AUTHOR: DIANNE WARTH-VEREEN

kidnapped that little girl from the Towne
Creek mound site? I sure wish she would
come up with an answer to Harry's death.
Right now about all I can attribute it to is heat
stroke or food poisoning from that hot dog he
had been eating and both of those have been
ruled out."

Nancy walked C.J. down the hall to the
Sheriff's office and then went up street to
Watson's for a vanilla Coke. She stopped off to
pick up her mail at the post office; stuck her
head in Leggett's to say hello to Mary and
then slowly made her way back to the
courthouse to finish out her day. The
temperature on the Waccamaw Bank
thermometer said that the day had already
topped 97 degrees. July and August were
always the hottest months in Southport. What
she wouldn't give for a dip in a swimming pool.
Instead, she answered the ringing cell phone
in her pocket as she went through the door
into the courthouse building.

"Dudley! You bad cat!" she addressed the large
gray and white tom cat that was waddling
toward her with a satisfied look on his face.
"Miss Susie is looking for you." She picked the
heavy cat up and tucked him under her arm.
"You have to stop running off like this. One of

these days someone is going to pick you up
and keep you." The big cat looked chastened
for a minute and then settled down to be
carried. Nancy headed out the courthouse and
up Moore Street towards Susie's house to
return the naughty cat. Kids kept stopping her
to pet Dudley. He was a big town favorite. By
the time she made it to Susie's house, Nancy's
arm was tired from holding the fifteen pound
cat to keep him from escaping again.

"Oh, you found him! Thank you, Nancy. Where
was he?" Susie held the big cat in her lap as
she and Nancy sat down to enjoy a glass of tea.

"He was outside Miss Vickie's office, as usual.
She must have brought him something back
from lunch. You know what a traveling
gourmet that cat is."

"I know what a furry monster he is, too. " She
stood and dumped Dudley out of her lap as she
brushed off her black slacks. Cat hair flew
everywhere. "I don't think Dudley has a
shedding season," she said. "He is an equal
opportunity shedder." Nancy laughed because
it was well known that Dudley was the cause
of many a sneeze around town.

"What was the thing you think you might have

AUTHOR: DIANNE WARTH-VEREEN

found?"

"It's just a few hairs that were found in Harry's lungs. They were embedded in the tiny little alveoli. The last autopsy before the body was turned over to his parents found them. No one was sure what they were."

"What did they look like? Did it look like a woman's hair?"

Nancy laughed the deep throated laugh that she had inherited from her father, Quack. "No, it wasn't a woman's hair. It would sure clear things up if it was. They were little short hairs; kinda grayish." She looked down and saw a few of the hairs on Susie's pants. "Kinda like *that*," she said as she pointed at the hairs on her pants.

"*DUDLEY*!" They both said the word at the same time. "You don't suppose..." Susie said as she reached for a fabric softener sheet to remove the cat hair.

" It's possible," said Nancy. "I will take some of these to compare to the ones the guy at Chapel Hill pulled out of Harry's lungs. Do you think Dudley could have been anywhere around Harry the day of the parade?"

AUTHOR: DIANNE WARTH-VEREEN

"Who knows? Was he home that day?"

"No, in fact, I found him up near the park and got one of the kids in my Sunday school class to take him home."

"What if he somehow found his way into the car where Harry was sitting?"

"***THAT'S IT!*** " Susie shouted so loudly that Nancy jumped and nearly fell over. "I know what killed Harry Tomkins!" She smiled a little smile that reminded Nancy of all the photos she had seen of the Mona Lisa. She had always thought that woman had a deep dark secret. Now Susie had that same look.

"What? Don't keep me in suspense; tell me. How did Harry die? What do you know that two coroners and a medical examiner havent been able to figure out?"

"The hairs in Harry's lungs; they must be Dudley's. When Harry was a little boy he was had terrible asthma and I think he also had a lot of allergies. One was a *cat* allergy."

"You might have something there, Miss Susie. Let's take a trip down to the lab and do a little comparison."

AUTHOR: DIANNE WARTH-VEREEN

They walked back up the street to the courthouse where Nancy had her lab. She has brought the hairs off Susie's slacks with her to compare to the ones she already had that were in Harry's lungs. They put both sets under the high powered electric microscope that was the center of the lab and Nancy pronounced them a match.

"Now, what do we think happened," she asked Miss Susie?

"I think that Dudley got away from that little Faulk boy and followed the scent of food up to the hospital parking lot. Harry was eating hotdogs and you know how much Dudley likes those. He probably got into the car while Harry was eating and had a little lunch. Maybe he even got up under Harry's nose. You know how he likes to rub on people and if they aren't paying attention to him he will get in someone's face. That could explain how the hair got in his lungs. Could that have killed him?"

"Basically, I suppose, it is possible. If Harry was terribly allergic then Dudley rubbing in his face could have caused an allergy or asthma attack so severe that his bronchial tubes would have gone into spasm. Lack of oxygen, spasms, histamine reactions and asphyxia. Combined with the heat of the day, eating; it's possible. Miss Susie, I think you did it! I am going to call C.J. and have her come over to hear the theory.

Fourteen

After all the facts were checked and re-checked, it was indeed determined that Harry had died of an asthma or allergy attack caused by a histamine reaction to cat hair. The items found in the car at the time of death included a partially eaten hotdog with tooth marks that resembled Dudley's. Miss Susie had remembered Harry's allergy to cat hair and his parents confirmed that it was an extreme one. The case was officially marked closed and C.J. was happy to put it away.

C.J. called Sparkie to tell her the verdict. The conversation was less than enlightening. C.J. had expected Sparkie to admit that Harry was her daughter's father but that didn't happen. She just said she was glad the mystery had

AUTHOR: DIANNE WARTH-VEREEN

been solved. Perhaps it was best for everyone that Harry Tomkins just remain dead and buried.

Miss Susie was suddenly the toast of the town. She had once again solved an unsolvable case that had stymied all the experts. Dudley was restricted to a new screened in back porch so that he wouldn't be roaming all over town. Miss Susie called it "house arrest" and said it was his sentence for causing Harry's death. Dudley didn't care as long as he had plenty of food. Miss Susie figured that Dudley's "cat logic" was working so that he actually thought he was being rewarded so he preened whenever guests came by the house (which they often did to discuss how she had solved the mystery). Everyone was referring to Miss Susie as Southport's Mrs. Fletcher or Miss Marple. At least everyone agreed it was a strange "murder" case. A group of them were sitting at a table at Quack's for lunch discussing everything that had happened. A toast was made to Miss Susie with large, frosty glasses of sweet tea. Everyone agreed that, sometimes, THE FOURTH OF JULY CAN BE MURDER.

AUTHOR: DIANNE WARTH-VEREEN

Afterword

Susie Carson died in September of 2008 at the age of 88. She suffered a recurrence of her breast cancer which had been in remission until the last year of her life. Although she gave birth to only one child, her daughter Kathryn, Susie had many "children" who took time in the final months to help care for her so that she could remain in the home she loved with her family and friends beside her. (Thank you "adopted kids" Joe, Ruthie, Andy, Nancy, Barbara, Dianne; all those who worked with and for Kathryn and Arnold to maintain the home like Harriett and Jennifer and others; family members: sister Thelma Dunn and family, brother William Sellers' family; {apologies to anyone I may have forgotten to mention, you were very special to Susie and us}

"Miss Susie" left a legacy that includes helping found the Southport Historical Society, her Star News newspaper column " A Bit of History", her books on local history and about her mother, Leila Jane (known to many of us as Big Mama), her local history class at the Community College that allowed so many new comers and locals to learn about the history of Southport and Brunswick County,

AUTHOR: DIANNE WARTH-VEREEN

and her genealogy classes that helped people discover their roots. A yearly scholarship is awarded to a deserving Brunswick Co. high school senior in her memory by the Southport Historical Society. The proceeds of the Susie Carson mystery series will be added to that fund.

I am proud to say that I was part of her "family". Her sister, Thelma, was one of my mother's best friends. I was named Susan in Miss Susie's honor and she was my godmother, my mentor, and my surrogate mother after the death of my own. Her daughter, Kathryn, is my "sister", my of my oldest and best friends. I promised Miss Susie in her last days that I would make her the heroine of a mystery series devoted to the Southport/Brunswick County area and its history and stories. She feared no one would be left to tell the stories that had always interested her about the area. Miss Susie and Mr. Jimmy Wolfe, Miss Leila Piggot were our local story tellers and they all are now gone.

Miss Susie, you are missed every day.

AUTHOR: DIANNE WARTH-VEREEN

THE SUSIE CARSON HISTORY

MYSTERIES

We hope this series will be popular and help promote the scholarship given in Miss Susie's honor.

In the coming books we plan to explore more Southport and Brunswick Co. history as well as a little North Carolina history. We will also venture into genealogy. These subjects were dear to Susie and make for an interesting subject for a mystery.

I will continue to speak of locals who have left us as well as those who are with us still. I will also continue to merge the past with the present to the confusion of those who are not locals.

AUTHOR: DIANNE WARTH-VEREEN

THE SUSIE CARSON HISTORY

MYSTERIES

AUTHOR: DIANNE WARTH-VEREEN

THE SUSIE CARSON HISTORY

MYSTERIES

AUTHOR: DIANNE WARTH-VEREEN